Cover by George Cotronis

Material from this book first appeared in short stories first published in these venues:

"Charlie Harmer's Last Request" in the Book of Dead Things anthology

"Charlie Harmer Looks Back" and "Charlie Harmer's Day Off" in the Pseudopod fiction podcast

Dedicated to the memory of my friend Ben Hyink. We talk all the time, but I still miss you.

Charlie Harmer Takes A Ride

by Brendan Detzner

CHAPTER 1

Mark and Harry had the radio turned up just loud enough to hear. Not the music, just the noise and some of the words.

"This is Charlie Harmer on WBLI classic radio, joining you on a wonderful Monday night…"

Harry sat in the passenger seat watching the barrier fence bounding the edge of the Interstate roll by.

It was dark; the streetlights loomed overhead like vultures, continuing at regular intervals ahead and behind them as far as they could see, leaving only a thin black space between each one. The fuel gauge had been hovering near empty for a few miles now, but there was no use pointing it out to Mark. He always let things ride to the last minute. It was just how he was.

A cop appeared in the rearview mirror. Mark took a quick glance at the back seat. Old books with leather covers, road maps, tapes, photo negatives. Most of the bad stuff was in the trunk: pills, a candy tin full of weed, a fancy silver knife Mark saw in a head shop in San Francisco and insisted had something to it. There was also a gun in the back of the glove compartment. Supposedly it was for emergencies, but they really kept it just for the thrill of having it.

Nothing was out in the open.

The cop went past them and disappeared over the horizon.

"We really ought to find a hotel," Harry said.

Mark didn't answer.

Harry wondered how tired he was, it was impossible to tell through the sunglasses. For all Harry knew, he was already sleeping and just kept his hand steady on the wheel through force of habit.

Finally Mark said something. "Yeah. I'll get off at the next exit and we'll look around."

Harry leaned back in his seat. "Great."

"I don't know why we keep coming back to Chicago," Mark said.

Harry closed his eyes. "We had some luck last time."

"We saw an old woman pushing a shopping cart."

"Her head was in the cart."

They'd seen better. They'd taken notes and snapped pictures, bragged about it on the Internet; they'd met like that, Mark and Harry and a few others. In Cleveland, they sat on a piano player's grave and heard music, and in Jacksonville they'd watched a tree bleed. They'd walked through the front door of an abandoned house in the middle of nowhere in Iowa and woken up two days later on the front porch, naked, with their hands around each other's throats.

At the beginning of the trip there'd been half a dozen people, but that had been months ago. Now there was only the two of them, and Harry was thinking about just pulling the plug on the whole thing and going home. It had been a long time since his parents had died. It wasn't that he felt any better, this just wasn't helping anymore.

They came to an exit. The Beach Boys were singing about summer. They ran out of lyrics and the song faded out in perfect harmony.

They found a hotel and got a room. They went in; Harry fell down on the covers. A minute later, he was sleeping soundly. Mark waited by the door until he was sure Harry wasn't moving.

He stepped back outside and got into the car. He reached into his hip pocket, found a black thread, and pulled. The thread had a small teardrop crystal hanging from it. He tied the crystal to his rearview mirror. It looked like something you'd buy from a hippie at a flea market.

He started the engine, pulled out of the parking lot, and got back on the highway. The crystal began to spin gently, back and forth. The streetlights overhead shone through the glass, casting tiny slices of green and yellow light on the dashboard.

He turned up the radio. For a moment he wondered if he had the wrong station; he heard a piano playing what sounded like classical music. He reached tentatively for the dial, not sure where to go.

But then a girl started talking, slowly and just out of rhythm with the music, something about wanting to dance, her parents not liking her boyfriend's motorcycle, fifties greaser shit with a wall of sound behind it. He pressed a button on the dash and set the trip odometer to zero.

The song ended, and the DJ started talking.

“Charlie Harmer here on WBLI classic radio, glad to have you here with me on a Tuesday morning. It’s too early for the farmers, so I just want to say hi to all of you out there in radio-land on the tail end of a good time and thank you for spending it here with us. If you’ve got anything to say, all you have to do is speak up and say hello. In the meantime we’ve got another great set of music…”

Mark realized the DJ hadn’t given a phone number.

“Hello?” he whispered hesitantly.

“Glad to hear from you son,” the voice on the radio said. “What’s your name?”

“Mark.”

"Mark with a C or Mark with a K?"

"With a K," Mark said, and felt silly.

“Nice to meet you Mark, I’m Charlie. You sure seem surprised for somebody who went to so much trouble to get in touch with me.”

“But…” Mark tried to think how to say it. “You’re not dead.”

“I sure am, for twenty-five years now. But still broadcasting. Did you get the crystal from Billy?”

Mark nodded.

“So you know what the rules are, right?”

Billy told Mark the rules when he gave him the crystal: Hang it from the rearview mirror, have your radio tuned to the right frequency. Travel for twenty miles, and don’t drop below the speed limit.

“I know the rules,” Mark said.

“That’s good. Speed limit here’s fifty-five. You’re really going to want to be careful about that.”

“Do I tell you who I want to talk to?”

"The way it works is that you only talk to me. But I can pass a message along to whoever you want and tell you what they have to say back to you."

Mark reached into the back seat with his right hand and pulled out a notebook and pen. There wasn't much light, but he managed to make out the first name on the list.

"A man named John Burris robbed a bank about twenty years ago. They caught him a few days later, but they never recovered the money. He died in prison. I want to know where he hid it."

"It'll take a little while to patch through."

"How long?"

"Not really sure. Wouldn't mind chatting a little bit in the meantime though. I don't get to talk to people much."

Mark didn't want to talk, but he didn't want to upset whatever it was that was talking to him.

"All right."

The odometer turned over, eight miles had gone past.

"Thanks. Last person who got in touch was Billy. How is Billy?"

Billy was an old man Mark met in a bar in St. Louis. He was fat and wore a plain red baseball cap and had trouble speaking in complete sentences. Mark had figured him for a drunk, but he went to the bar several times and never saw Billy drinking that much, definitely not enough to account for how fried he was. If he hadn't heard him muttering something about dead people, Mark never would have given him a second thought.

"He looked pretty messed up."

Charlie sighed. The sound was a low rush passing through the speakers.

"Yeah, well. Fifty-five, Mark, be careful. So tell me something else. Most people don't seek out ghosts, how did you get interested in doing something like that?"

"I saw some people die in a traffic accident."

The speakers were silent. Mark was offended; he felt like that deserved a reaction. "Are you still there?"

"You bet. Just took a second for John to come through. He buried the money in a forest preserve." Charlie gave him the directions. It wouldn't be too hard to find the spot.

He checked the next name.

"Al Capone. There's got to be something."

The trip odometer hit eleven.

There were more names on the list. Charlie wanted to know how some baseball teams were doing. Mark didn't know anything about baseball, but he was able to fake his way through it.

"I was kind of hoping I could ask you what it's like to be dead," Mark said.

"I'm not a poet." It was the first time Charlie sounded anything less than friendly. "Another one's coming. This one's complicated. Get ready."

Mark spent almost five minutes writing as fast as he could. He finished one sheet, turned to the next one, and filled about two-thirds of the page before he was done.

"All right," Mark said. "Thanks."

"No problem, but I think you're running out of road."

"Just one more. The name of the guy I've been traveling with is Harry Lund. His parents died a little over a year ago.

"It'd speed things up if I knew how they died."

"A traffic accident."

He waited for Charlie's answer, but the speakers were quiet. Slowly, music filled the car, the volume started low and gently crept up. A simple song with three chords.

"You make my heart sing..."

The car was moving at sixty miles an hour. Mark cut back on the gas very slightly. The dial on the speedometer dropped down and hovered between the white lines above the fifty-five mark. By the time the song was done, the odometer was halfway through its seventeenth mile. Charlie's voice came back over the radio.

"I'm sorry, but you're going to have to pass on this one. By the time they come around, you'll be out of time."

Mark slowed the car down to forty. For a moment, everything was quiet except for the sound of the wheels turning underneath them.

"You really shouldn't do that. It's not going to buy you enough time anyway…"

Mark pulled over to the side of the road and put the car in park.

"You're making a huge mistake."

"Just let me know when I can talk to Harry's parents."

A minute passed in silence.

"All right, they're here."

"Tell them that I apologize." Mark pulled back onto the road.

"I told them, they heard it."

Mark watched as the speedometer rose past thirty-five. He heard a siren. He looked in his rearview mirror and saw spinning lights behind him.

"Is that a cop?" Mark asked, and immediately felt like an idiot, and anyway he got no answer. He pulled over. The police car pulled up behind him, and a large man got out and walked down the side of the road. He was hard to see. Even from only a few feet away, he was still only a black shape, a pair of shoulders floating in the air.

Mark rolled down the window. "Is there a problem?"

"The speed limit is fifty-five."

"I was going forty."

The man outside the window nodded. "That's too slow. There's a fine."

"How much?"

"It's not that kind of a fine. Step out of the car."

Mark pictured Billy, sitting at the bar dead sober but still muttering to himself, his eyes wandering aimlessly around the room.

He took a deep breath and forced himself to forget. Fear was a signal. Once you heard what it had to tell you, there was no point keeping it around.

"You're going to be needing my registration, right?"

The man outside raised his hand hesitantly, like he was about to say something. Mark reached into the glove compartment. He spun back around with his arms outstretched and the gun in his hand. He pulled the trigger three times.

The sound was like a hammer smacking against his eardrums; he didn't feel anything else until a moment after. His wrists were sore, and he could smell smoke in the air. He looked out the window and saw something on the ground a few yards away that looked like a pile of black felt.

The speakers came back to life with a hum of low static. "I've got to say, I've never seen anybody try that before. Won't kill him, though."

The pile began to stir. Mark saw hands pressing against the ground, shoulders rising into the air.

"He'll catch you."

The car gently lurched forward as Mark shifted gears.

"Wait," Charlie said.

Mark stomped on the brakes without thinking.

"Check his car."

Mark stayed frozen in place. He kept his feet pinned down, one on the clutch and the other on the brake. Each one felt like it had a jackrabbit inside of it trying to get out. He didn't know what to do.

Fuck it.

He shifted to reverse and pulled back alongside the cop car. He got out, ran over to it, and stuck his arm through the window. It was dark inside and cold like a meat locker. He reached toward the steering wheel and felt something metallic, and when he pulled his arm free of the window, there was a car key in his hand.

He looked up the road. The man he'd shot was on his feet, standing tall, lit up by the headlights. It was a cop; he was wearing a blue uniform. He had three fresh bullet holes in his chest and another much older one right between his eyes.

Mark ran around his car as fast as he could and climbed into the driver's seat.

He hit the gas pedal; the tires shrieked as the car cut across the lanes. A shot was fired, then another, behind him now. He straightened out the wheel and pressed down on the gas pedal.

He just went and went, and soon the man shooting at him was gone, a tiny black shape in the rearview mirror getting harder and harder to see.

It was just a key. It didn't have a logo. It looked like a spare you'd have made at the hardware store.

"He won't get too far without that," Charlie said.

Mark didn't say anything. He looked at the odometer. Eighteen miles had gone past.

"On the other hand, he has no problem walking for a long time, and he doesn't like people stealing his things."

Mark shrugged. "I'll figure something out."

"That's the spirit, I guess. So tell me something…"

Mark reached for the volume.

"That's no way to treat somebody who just did you a favor. It's kind of funny, you killing somebody in a car accident and your travel buddy's parents dying in a car accident."

Mark put his hand back down on his knee and kept steering with the other one.

"I said there was an accident," he whispered. "I didn't say anything about killing anybody."

"I've heard both sides of the story now, Mark. Does your friend know?"

Mark didn't answer.

"All that time on the road and you never told him?"

Still nothing.

"All right, then."

The odometer turned over. Nineteen miles.

"Did they accept my apology?" He was still whispering.

"Sure. Dead people get to be pretty understanding about this kind of stuff. They just hope that you're a little more careful in the future. We've about reached the end of your ride, is there anybody else you want me to try and ring up real fast?"

Mark shook his head. "No." He looked down at the key again. "Are you going to be in some kind of trouble?"

Charlie laughed. "It's a little late to be worrying about that. Trip's almost done anyway. Let me play you a song."

Music filled the car, three men singing in harmony and snapping their fingers. The odometer hit twenty.

The next exit was a cloverleaf. Mark got off and went back the way he'd come. By the time he reached the place where he'd been pulled over, he could see sunlight in his rearview mirror.

He went back to the hotel, took the notebook with him to the room, and put it on the table by the window. He opened it, took a pen out of his pocket, and wrote in the margin.

HARRY—

HERE YOU GO. IT'S BEEN A GOOD TRIP.

Then, after thinking for a second:

I'M SORRY

—MARK

He looked over the notes. If even half the tips were good, and Harry followed up on them, he'd be set for life. Mark threw the car keys down on top of the notebook and left.

There was a gas station next to the motel they were staying at, and on the far side of the station was a pay phone with a Yellow Pages on top. He flipped through it, found the number of a cab company, and gave them a call.

He found himself playing the accident over in his head while he waited. It was something he used to do all the time, but he hadn't done it for a while. He'd been a little drunk; when he made the turn he saw the headlights coming, and he knew it was going to be close, but he'd been sure he'd just make it, just close enough to give the other guy a jolt without their cars ever touching. When he woke up in the hospital and heard what had happened, his first reaction was to get angry at how unfair it all was. A few inches difference and he'd have been fine.

The cab arrived. Mark climbed into the back seat. The radio was on.

"This is WBLI classic radio. Charlie Harmer isn't going to be with us for awhile, but I hope you'll stay tuned, we have a lot of great music coming your way…"

She played a song older than the ones he'd been hearing, a woman with a deep voice and an orchestra behind her.

"So where are you headed?" the driver asked him.

CHAPTER TWO

1

It all starts again, and I'm sitting across from Margie in Jack's restaurant. It's late, maybe two o'clock in the morning, which might not seem so crazy to you, but this was Milwaukee, not New York or Paris or someplace, and even in New York or Paris two o'clock used to be a lot later than it is now. I don't think you could be out as late as me and Margie were that night, not anymore.

This place is a refuge, and not just because there aren't any other customers. Any two people that wanted to sit together in Jack's restaurant, that was fine with Jack. He had a shotgun under the counter for anybody that wanted to argue with him. I never found out why he was like that, you'd never know it looking at him, he was an old guy, not some kind of radical. He was bald and wore a white smock all the time. Just a guy, like you see everywhere.

Even in an empty restaurant with friendly management, we're sitting all the way in the back. We don't even notice; hiding comes naturally to both of us. I'm making her laugh. She's nervous, being out so late, being alone with me, but I'm making her feel better, I'm doing a good job. Talking to her I don't even see her, not really. I'm thinking about her sister, thanking me. Seeing me in a new light, in her gratitude. Thinking about me the way I think about her. I fantasize. There are few limits to the things I think about her saying or doing, even sitting across the table from her little sister in a restaurant.

At some point I compliment her latest record, her first record. She blushes. She tells me that it was just an experiment, a silly little thing. She's happy to back up her sister, she loves being a Bluebird. I make fun of her loyalty, a little bit but not too much. I find the line and I walk right on it. My special talent. She's still laughing.

I pay for the meal- there's no alternative, it was just what a man did- and we leave. From the moment we leave our safe haven everything becomes uncertain. We're not far from where she lives, it's maybe a twenty minute walk; I should take that walk with her, but at the same time our late night is on the verge of becoming early morning, and we're not in Jack's restaurant anymore. I want to be her knight in shining armor. On the other side of the scale is reality, and the hundreds of pairs of eyes between here and there.

She makes it easy on me. She's leaning away, separating, saying goodbye. I am simultaneously relieved and insulted. I'm still projecting myself into the future, thinking about what big sister is going to think.

That's what's on my mind when little Margie kisses me on the cheek. I try to figure out what the hell just happened. She walks away and is gone.

The dream goes back the way it came, a swinging pendulum. I'm back inside the restaurant and the whole thing starts again, like it's been doing for a long time, like it probably always will. This is it, my place in the grand scheme of things.

Sometimes I get a little time off.

2

The dream fades away. The boss is coming. She graciously gives me time to collect myself. We're in some kind of a lounge; everything is upholstered with vertical stripes and there are flaming torches on the walls. The boss is not big on context, sometimes. I don't hold it against her, she's a busy lady.

It's really warm in here.

The smell of sulfur fills the air and vanishes, and she's sitting in front of me. She's wearing a red dress and has long brown hair; you want to go swimming in it, you imagine it cool against your skin like water.

"You're staring, Charlie," she says.

"I'm sorry, I can't help myself. I didn't think I'd have the chance to see you again."

I had a regular job not too long ago, but I did something I shouldn't have and lost it. She fired me, but never got upset. She's never all that surprised when people do things they shouldn't.

"You must've known it would happen sooner or later."

"I don't know anything for sure, beautiful. All I can do is hope."

I smile and she smiles back. We talk for a while. She's got a lot on her mind, work stuff. I don't know why she tells me things. I guess it makes her feel better, the same way it makes anybody feel better to get something off their chest.

She finally gets around to it. "There's something I was hoping you could do for me."

"Anything you need. I'm grateful you would ask, after last time."

"This is just a small favor. A chance to pick yourself back up."

She tells me what the favor is. I'm surprised.

"It's a little more personal than I'm used to."

"If you'd rather not do it, I understand."

My only alternative to not doing what she asks is going back where I came from. The boss is far beyond having to threaten people to get what she wants.

"Not at all," I say. "I'd be happy to."

It feels like I'm falling.

3

I'm dropped off on a street corner. It's nighttime; the sky overhead has a gentle orange glow that swallows the stars. The houses stand apart from each other but there's not much space in between them, no driveways. The lots are deeper than they are wide. I glance over the picket fences as I walk north and see birdbaths, fountains, rock gardens, flower arrangements, carefully arranged little stone paths. One private world after another.

I hear a preacher's voice booming from a couple of blocks away. It bounces off the surrounding buildings; I can only make out every other word of what he's saying. To the side of the twin front doors of the church is a faded metal plaque; pinned to the wall above them with bungee cords is a white tarp with giant block letters announcing the new name of the mission and what times services are held. I pause for a second to admire the performance. I wonder what would happen if I tried to go inside.

A stray cat limps nervously across the street as I reach the end of the neighborhood. I'm faced with a four-lane road that's mostly empty of traffic. On the other side is a giant strip mall with a grocery store and shops and a couple of those big box places where you can buy anything. A giant parking lot stretches out far and deep, left and right; I turn my head and see my destination, a fortress in red neon. It's actually smaller than the buildings surrounding it but by night it seems to tower over everything.

As I get closer, I see more of the restaurant. It's in the style of Jack's old place, but nothing actually like it, too big, too out in the open. Even this time of night, there's a line of cars leading up to the drive-in window and a crew of men and women and teenagers in black polo shirts approaching each car and writing down their orders so they can run them straight to the kitchen and keep things moving quickly.

I go in and I don't know what to think. It's no one thing, it's many things, stacked on top of each other. It's crowded and it's loud. There are posters from old movies on the walls hanging next to autographed pictures of nominally famous people on the walls. There are records hanging from the ceiling, little seven inch singles printed on transparent red vinyl. There's a jukebox next to the door but it's only a decoration, it doesn't work. A Temptations song is playing over the PA.

It's like somebody threw a party amongst the wreckage that had been my life. It's strange and it's painful, but I'm glad somebody's having a good time.

There's a set of three parallel lines leading up to the cash register, and a packed crowd filling the open space in the far corner of the room. The people standing behind the cash registers are all black, but the rest of the restaurant is a mix of everything with everything, teenagers with brightly colored jackets crammed three deep into booths, families, couples. I see a pudgy man in a brown suit looking down at a small child, his son, as they wait for their number to get called. Standing behind him is an aggressively skinny black girl in a bright white winter coat with a logo I don't recognize on the collar and a pink cell phone in her ear. She looks around, changing the way the light hits her face, and I realize that she might be a little older than she's dressing. The girl standing behind her is the opposite. Her mouth is a thin horizontal line stretched across her face. She's centered; she looks like someone who's lived, but she's just a kid, part of a trio, the three of them whispering to each other in Spanish. One of her friends is glancing back at a boy at the end of the line; he's wearing all black, everything creased and clean and perfect, an oversized baseball cap cocked to one side on top of his head. He is constantly looking, evaluating, thinking, letting everybody know he's thinking. He notices her and switches up just long enough to smile. He's a good-looking guy. I imagine he gets this a lot.

I see the kid I'm looking for on the other side of the room. Another teenager, slender but not skinny exactly. He's wearing a pair of pre-faded-jeans and a dark blue hooded sweatshirt. His hair shines, he works at it. I want to say that he's Mexican, but I can't claim to be sure. What's funny is that there's something about him that seems British to me, like skinny rock-and-roll British. Maybe his nose, it makes him look like Roger Daltrey. One of the girls behind the counter calls out his number and he picks up his Italian beef. He sits down at an empty booth and unwraps his sandwich, but he doesn't eat, he just looks at it. There's something on his mind.

I sit down. It takes a second for him to notice.

"I'm eating alone." Not loud, not being a tough guy. Just saying it.

I snap my fingers. The music stops and a new song starts playing. There's a woman singing softly over a rhythm section. A piano sneaks in sideways. No one notices the change except him. He takes a closer look at me, at my face.

But there is no face.

"You seem like a nice guy that's thinking about doing something that would surprise people," I say.

She's still singing. Her voice is innocent, sounding out each note the best way she knows how, and simultaneously drenched in sex. She knows something deeper then the words, but she doubts you'll ever be worthy of knowing what it is.

I snap my fingers again. All activity ceases- every single person in the restaurant stops what they're doing and stares into space. People from the line turn in the direction of our booth and move forward, stepping on stage. The man in the brown suit and the woman in the white coat and the girl that's too serious for her age and the boy in the hat.

"The woman singing this song right now was named Beverly Blue. When I first met her I was a disc jockey at a radio station in Milwaukee."

The girl becomes somebody else. Her carriage changes; she doesn't have to be defensive any more, she's royalty, she's King Kong in a cocktail dress and high heels.

"The group she was in was called the Bluebirds. She was the big deal in the group, her little sister backed her up along with another girl they kept replacing."

The woman in the white coat changes too, but draws less attention to herself, the little beat coming after the big one. She's young again, and it's less fun then she remembers. She's a mouse. She shrinks.

"Beverly and her sister and her boyfriend all lived together in a house on the opposite side of town from where I lived. Her boyfriend was their manager. Their everything, really."

The man in the brown suit comes back to life. Something rises up inside him, something that had long since been burned away by long years of fidelity and devotion to his children, if he'd ever had it at all. Everything that he looks at, it seems possible that he might want to eat alive, and yet he is polite in his way, stylish. You want him to like you, even against your better judgment.

"My father owned a little independent label, along with a couple of record stores and a recording studio." The kid with the baseball cap has become my father, but has done so without announcing himself, which was my father's style. "None of it ever made him much real money, but that was never the point. He rented jukeboxes to people too. If you wanted your bar to stay open, you rented a jukebox from my father and paid whatever he told you the price was. That's how I thought of him. He was the jukebox guy."

The four of them move into the open space by the front door. The other customers sleepwalk out of the way, pressing against each other to make room.

The kid with the big nose watches. He is appropriately scared out of his wits.

"I don't know exactly how it is that the Bluebells came to record on my father's label. Money probably changed hands, more than that I'm not sure about. I was there when they first recorded. My dad wanted me there, he didn't trust his own taste in music as much as he did mine. This time he didn't really need me. We both knew what we had."

They take position on the floor, my dad on one side, the Bluebells on the other standing behind their manager as he makes his pitch, Beverly sly and smiling and Marjorie scared and wrapped up in herself like a raccoon in a hole. My father listens, evaluating every word carefully but still relaxed, not really throwing his whole self into it. This is a hobby, something he does to relax.

Beverly leans forward and opens her mouth, moving her lips in time with the music into a microphone that isn't there. Her boyfriend moves to the side with the others, smiling, satisfied. My father is standing next to him. Margie is standing by herself in the corner, staring into the booth, jealous, afraid.

"We could have run into trouble getting it on the radio, but Dad owned the radio. We could've had trouble getting it in stores, but nobody running a record store was going to argue with my father if he had a record he wanted them to carry. So it

got heard, and it was a hit. But it was just a local hit, the kind of hit we'd had before."

Beverly's boyfriend leans over and whispers in my father's ear.

"This song wanted to be more than that. It wanted to be national. But making that happen wasn't going to be such an easy thing from a business point of view."

The four of them sat down cross-legged on the floor. No chairs, no dinner tables, no plates, no silverware. Only ghosts. They move like marionettes, their hands lowering to the floor and rising up to their mouths.

"That was when I really got to know Beverly. When my father went into business with someone in a partners kind of a way, he always really wanted them to feel like family. He didn't have it in him to trust anybody he hadn't cooked a meal for."

The others get up and move off stage, except for Beverly, who stays where she is. She stares blankly into space. Her song is still playing.

"I fell for her pretty hard. At the time, I wasn't really able to admit it to myself. You've got to understand, just having them over for dinner was enough to get people talking behind my father's back, that was how things were. And I was not a brave man. But it's easy to see, in hindsight. She really was gorgeous."

Beverly stands up and moves back, my father steps forward and sits down where she just was. He's whispering into the phone the way another man would yell. His eyes have shrunk down into dull metal points. He is very, very upset.

He gets up and Beverly walks back into the center of the open space. She starts talking but there's no voice, only her lips moving. She's looking at you. You're the one that she wants. That thing you were hoping for, that you would never admit to anyone, that you embarrassed yourself just daydreaming about, is happening, right now, right before your eyes.

"One of the problems with getting a national hit was getting national distribution. There was no good way to do it. You could get a deal with one big distributor and hope it decided to

pay you what it said it was going to pay you, or you could run around and line up a bunch of little distributors and hope half of them gave you what you needed to pay your lawyers and sue the other half. My dad wasn't really used to getting pushed around, so he went with one of the big companies. Somehow he got pushed around anyway; why he didn't go to war over that, what kind of leverage they had, I don't know, but they weren't going to pay up until we had another hit on the same level as the first one.

"While that was going on, Beverly approached me asking to borrow some money. She owed somebody and she didn't want my dad to know about it, but she said that she knew I'd understand. It doesn't sound like much, but I had an overactive imagination, I thought it meant more than it did."

Her face goes blank. She takes a step back and the stage is empty.

"They dropped off the face of the earth, all three of them. They got an offer from another label in New York and decided to make a break for it. My money got them a new car and some gas."

Beverly and her agent step forward again. They kneel down on the floor and put their hands behind their backs. They look up and start crying. Beverly's boyfriend begs for mercy.

"They didn't make it that far. My dad pulled me to the side a couple of weeks later and told me that his people had found them. It was just a whisper in my ear, more then I usually ever got to hear about my father's business. But I wanted even more than that. I wanted to pull the trigger."

The music stops. Beverly's boyfriend's head kicks back and his body slumps over. Beverly screams.

"As far as he was concerned, Beverly hadn't done anything wrong, or if she had he was willing to ignore it. He wanted her to keep singing. But she'd broken my heart."

Beverly's head kicks back in exactly the same way. She stops screaming and falls backwards. The music starts up again. My four actors return to their original positions with blank looks on their faces. Everyone in the restaurant suddenly restarts whatever it was they had been doing before I started telling my story. All was as it had been.

"My dad loved me. Anything I wanted, he gave me. That's it. That's my story."

The boy with the big nose looked over at where I'd put on my show, then back at me. He opened his mouth, but he couldn't put the words together.

"You want to know if I got away with it?" I ask. He nods. "I did. As far as anybody else was concerned Beverly was just one more girl who ran off to make the big time and never came back."

He finds his voice, sooner than most people would. He's a bold kid. He has something in him. I wonder if anyone's noticed, his parents, his teachers at school, anybody.

"You're not telling me the whole story."

"I've told you everything I knew at the time I died. Anything else would be speculation. But I do speculate. I'm dead, the way you'll be dead someday. All dead guys do is speculate."

I disappear. I'm still there, but he can't see me. He looks around, stares at the woman in the white coat while she continues to wait for her food, and leaves quickly, leaving his tray on the table.

I shovel his Italian beef into my mouth. I can feel something warm in my stomach, but the feeling quickly disappears as my surroundings fade away.

4

I'm back in the lounge. The brunette is sitting across from me.

"You did an excellent job, Charlie."

"I'm glad to hear it. I wasn't sure it was what you were looking for. It's not what I'd expected."

"What do you mean?"

"Whatever he was planning, it seems like it would be more your line to just let him do it."

"Maybe I need him for something later on."

"I guess you must." I look down at the floor. This is the difficult part. It's hard to be smooth while you're begging.

"Is there anything else you need done? I know you're not going to give me a regular job after last time, but if there's anything small that needs to happen, any little thing..."

She's smiling.

"Maybe later. Good night, Charlie. Thanks again."

And that's it. I'm back in the restaurant with Marjorie. She's talking about the record she just made. It was just an experiment, a silly little thing. She's happy to be a Bluebird.

I never found out what happened to Marjorie. After my father went to jail, I got another job in radio, a little station in Indianapolis. I don't know if she left town with her sister or if she got left behind. If she stayed in the music business, she either took a different name or was never that big a deal, because I never heard of her again.

I don't know what happened inside Margie's head that would cause her to develop a crush on a white guy ten years older than she was in the United States of America in 1958. I do know that her sister's boyfriend kept both of them pretty securely cooped up, and if she had any family other than her sister they weren't in the picture. She didn't know very many people. I might've been the only person who was nice to her on a regular basis.

I don't know if she knew, or could guess, or even suspected that I had anything to do with her sister's death. And if she did, I don't know what effect that knowledge would have had on her. I don't know what she was left with, after the two people who were her life's foundation suddenly disappeared.

She kisses me on the cheek, and walks away, and everything begins again. I wonder when the boss will need me again, I wonder who the boy with the big nose was and how his plans might have changed. I wonder how long it will be before the brunette summons all of her soldiers, calls in all her favors.

I am struck, not for the first time, with the irony of my situation. Praying to the devil for deliverance

CHAPTER THREE

Ashanda was only sentenced to a year, but she was locked up for almost six months longer than that, just because they didn't have any place for her to go, no foster placement willing or obligated to take her. She was sixteen years old when she finally got out. They pulled her out of Sunday school; she slid what was left of the granola bar the volunteers handed out every week into her sleeve and went to the counselor's office. When they told her she was leaving, her first thought was that they'd built a new prison.

Ashanda's aunt's name was Betty, and the last time Ashanda had seen her had been seven or eight years ago at Christmas. Her disappearance from the circle of people Ashanda knew and had contact with hadn't been a huge surprise. Ashanda's mother had a way of making people disappear. Then she disappeared.

It happened incredibly quickly, like a magic trick. Papers were signed, hands were shook, and suddenly Ashanda was standing in the parking lot. The clothes she'd arrived in didn't fit her anymore, so they'd given her a pair of jeans and a flannel shirt from the donations closet that made her look like a boy. Her aunt was wearing a long black dress with fringe on the bottom. Her hair was tied back; the clasp had a silver crescent moon on it.

She opened the door to her car.

"Let's get the hell out of here."

Ashanda got in and they left. They passed a furniture store and a patch of fast food restaurants; there were people walking through the parking lots, living their lives. Ashanda was upset. She remembered her trip here as a journey through the wilderness, from nowhere to nowhere. It bothered her that she'd let herself change how things had really been, that she'd lied to herself.

"I didn't know," Betty said, as they pulled onto the highway. "Nobody told me. I came as soon as I found out."

Ashanda didn't say anything.

They got off the highway. There was a cemetery on their left.

"There's a lot of cemeteries in Forest Park," Betty said. "The dead outnumber the living about ten to one."

Ashanda still didn't answer. She didn't know if she was being rude, or even whether or not she was angry. She didn't have the energy to sort through it. She burrowed deep into herself.

She was surprised when the car stopped. It was a yellow house. There was a sign hanging in the window.

PSYCHIC
TAROT READINGS
SPIRIT CONTACT
NO APPOINTMENTS AFTER MIDNIGHT

Along the bottom of the sign was a phone number.

Betty got out and climbed the stairs up to the front porch. Ashanda followed her. They went in. To the left was a small, spotlessly clean room with a table and two expensive-looking wooden chairs. The other doorway was blocked by a curtain. Betty pushed it away and went through to the kitchen. Ashanda followed her. The kitchen was completely free of any decoration; there were no magnets on the fridge, nothing on any of the counters except a phone.

"You must be hungry," Betty said. "I don't cook, but we can order whatever you'd like to have."

"Pizza," Ashanda said, the only thing she could think of.

"Sounds good." Betty dialed a number and ordered a pizza. Her voice was crisp and formal, polite without being warm.

Ashanda didn't like how Betty talked. She didn't like the kitchen, the way it looked like they were inviting people inside to buy the house. She decided she was going to run away. Not right now, but soon. There was no doubt in her mind.

The doorbell rang. Betty finished her order and hung up the phone angrily.

"This is not the time," she whispered under her breath. "This is not the time." She rubbed her eyes.

"I'm very sorry. I'm going to deal with this as quickly as I can." She gave Ashanda forty dollars. "If the pizza comes before I'm done pay for it and give the delivery person a tip. And if you could stay in the kitchen during the appointment I'd appreciate it. I haven't figured out how all this is going to work yet."

She went to the door. Ashanda listened from behind the curtain. She didn't really care what was happening. It was just something to do.

There was an elderly white woman in a purple track suit standing on the front porch.

"Oh hello, Betty, it's so good to see you."

"It's good to see you too, Ramona, but our appointment is for tomorrow. I'm not seeing anyone today."

"I was hoping you could make an exception. I'm sure it's all right with Robert. He's been acting up since last night, I think he wants to talk to me."

"All right, I'll what I can do, but I won't be able to spend a whole lot of time with you today."

"I understand."

They sat down at the round table. Betty's voice was serious, professional, the way Ashanda had heard nurses talk at the hospital.

"He's definitely here…" Betty said. "I can sense some strong feelings…"

"I just want to know why he's so angry. He's been so angry lately. I just hope it isn't anything I did."

"It might. It might not. Is there anyone else he might be angry with?"

"Jimmy… things have been going badly with Jimmy. He hasn't been doing very well in school."

They kept going like that. Betty mostly just asked questions. The angry one was her husband, Robert, who'd been dead for a while. Jimmy was their grandson.

Ashanda saw a man holding a pizza box approach the door. She made it outside before he could ring the doorbell, paid him, and made it back to the kitchen with the pizza. Betty's client didn't seem to notice.

"Why do you think Robert might feel that way?"

"The lung cancer… oh god no, you don't think Jimmy has it too? I always tell him he shouldn't smoke."

"There's no way to be sure. I sense that there's a threat. Whether it's already here or if it might be coming soon, I can't say and neither can Robert. But if you could persuade Jimmy to stop smoking, it couldn't hurt."

"I know, I know."

They got up. Ashanda waited a minute and peeked through the curtain. They were standing in the doorway.

"You have a special gift," Ramona said.

"I know," Betty answered. They hugged bloodlessly and Ramona put something in Betty's hand before she left. Betty closed the door. When she came back into the kitchen she was holding a roll of bills.

"I swear to god, if that woman wasn't made of money… I'm so sorry Ashanda. I wasn't supposed to be working today." She opened a pizza box and devoured a slice. "I thought she would never go."

"Is it real?" Ashanda blurted out.

Betty was about to reach for another slice of pizza when she heard the question.

"What do you mean?"

"Are you really like that? Do you have powers?"

Betty thought carefully before she said anything.

"What do you think, Ashanda?"

Ashanda didn't know what to do. She gave up. She said what she thought.

"I think it's bullshit. I think you lie."

Betty slowly smiled.

Betty and Ashanda talked about the business until the sun went down. It was Betty's favorite subject; she went over the rules, the rules within the rules, categories, distinctions, war stories.

"Somebody like Ramona, she's easy. I'm like a therapist for her, I just have to listen to her talk and take her money. The skill comes before that, it's what you need to put yourself in that position. It's about the state of mind they bring in through that door. You've got to ask questions. Your questions don't even have to be questions. They can be choices. Like, you get an image and you tell them about it. Maybe you got that image because of something that happened, maybe you got the image because it didn't happen. Either way, you win.

"The other thing to remember is that people are alike. Dogs are more different then people, Ashanda. Tell someone that they wear two faces, that people don't understand them. Tell anybody that. See what happens."

It wasn't very late, but Betty realized that Ashanda was falling asleep. She'd gotten carried away. It had been a long time since she'd been able to open up like this.

"I'm sorry," she said. "Watch me flap my mouth. You must be exhausted. Let me take you to your room."

They went upstairs. It wasn't a big room- the bed was huge, but it took up half of the available space. The closet was empty.

"I know we've got to get you some real clothes," Betty said. "I didn't want to buy anything without you."

Ashanda didn't answer.

"All right," Betty said. "I know it's been a long day. Good night, Ashanda."

Ashanda fell asleep right away and woke up three hours later. Her room. Her bed, her place to be. The room was dark, but not that dark, light crept in from the streetlight outside. Her door was closed. Her door. The privacy was thrilling and terrifying.

She heard a sound drift through her window and up the stairs of the house simultaneously. Someone pounding on the front door. She looked out the window. The man at the door was concealed from the neck up by the awning that covered the porch, and his sleeves were long, so that the hand he wasn't using to knock was concealed by the fabric. He was wearing a dark green military uniform that Ashanda didn't recognize. It was like something you'd see hanging on a mannequin in a museum.

She heard Betty go down the stairs, heard her voice as the door opened.

"You don't have an appointment."

The man at the door made a sound like air escaping from a tire and stepped inside the house. Ashanda heard Betty raise her voice.

"I'm not seeing anyone tonight. You need to leave. You need to leave."

Ashanda crept down the stairs, silently but as quickly as she could. She crawled on all fours to the kitchen doorway and snuck a look around the corner.

The man that had come through the door had a human skull where his face should have been.

She ducked back into the kitchen. Her eye caught the digital clock above the stove. It was ten minutes after midnight.

She heard them talking.

"Melissa… Melissa wants to talk to me."

"No…" Softer than before.

He hissed, and Ashanda heard something hit the wall. She peeked around the corner again and saw Betty crouched down on the floor, the man in the uniform towering over her. There was something wrong with her, even in the dark Ashanda could feel it. The man brought his arm down, as if to hit her. It never made contact, but Betty started shaking.

The man brought his hand back up and Ashanda could feel something inside of her being cut away, hollowed out. Her hope, dying.

She stepped into the hallway.

"Stop it."

The man in the uniform did stop. He turned in her direction.

"Who are you?" the man hissed.

Ashanda was unbowed. "Do you want to talk to Melissa or don't you?"

The man stepped back. He moved like a marionette- his body parts didn't seem to be connected to each other.

"You have the gift?" he whispered.

Ashanda didn't answer. Such questions were beneath her.

"How do I know?" the man continued, suspicious now.

"Melissa said that you were two people. When she was living. One for her and one for everybody else."

The man nodded, acknowledging the truth of what she'd said.

She tilted her head in the direction of the room with the round table. They went in together and sat down.

"What is she saying?" the man asked. "What is she trying to tell me?"

Ashanda closed her eyes and concentrated. "I see death. That's what she's showing me." She opened them again. "Yours and hers. Not at the same time though."

His jaw shook, his teeth rattled enthusiastically. "It was so hard, after she was gone."

"I'm seeing her when she was young."

The man nodded again. "She was hardly more then a girl when we were married."

"I see her. She's wearing a dress."

"Yes…" He tilted his head down towards the table.

"She's crying."

Ashanda wasn't sure why she'd said that. The man looked up. He rose from his seat smoothly and silently, as though he were carried by a gust of warm air.

"I never made my angel cry."

Ashanda looked directly into the man's empty eye sockets and did not blink.

"She's crying," Ashanda repeated.

The man's shoulders slumped. His teeth chattered gently and he looked to the side. "I never saw that. Even when…." He sat back down and exhaled. "More. I want more. Tell me."

They sat at the table for a little over an hour. Ashanda learned very little about the man she was speaking with. She gave him what he wanted, sunny days and dreams of children who were never born. Finally, the man in the uniform waved his hands.

"Enough… that's enough." He reached into his jacket, revealing what was left of his ribs. His hand emerged with a tiny round object, a coin. He put it down on the table.

He got up and so did Ashanda. He floated down the hall, his feet mock-walking slightly out of sync with the speed the rest of his body was traveling.

He opened the front door and stepped over Betty's body. She was still twitching; she was staring up at the ceiling. He stood in the doorway, lost in thought.

"It's so dull," he said. "It's cold and dark and nothing ever happens. And I'm alone. I thought that because I was a sinner, I knew where I was going; when she took her own life part of me was happy, because I knew the two of us would be in the same place."

He shrugged his shoulders. What are you gonna to do. He began to close the door, stopped, looked down at Betty, and waved his hand absentmindedly. She stopped moving. He went out onto the porch and slammed the door shut behind him.

Ashanda ran to her aunt. She dived down to the floor. Betty's skin was cold. She wasn't breathing. For a moment she was absolutely still.

Then she groaned, spasmed, breathed deeply and frantically. She reached out with her hands. The two of them held on to each other in the darkness of the hallway.

After a while, they got up. They went into the kitchen and turned on the lights.

"I hope that if this ever happens again, you'll be smart and run," Betty said. "The house has a back door."

She took a deep breath.

"You were very brave."

Ashanda wanted her to know that she hadn't been brave, that what she'd done had just come out of her naturally and that she still wasn't sure why she'd done it. But the words didn't arrive. They sat across from each other silently.

"Now is not the time for this," Betty finally said. "We'll talk in the morning."

They went back upstairs. Betty gave Ashanda a hug and they each went to bed.

Betty stayed in her room until she was as sure as she could be that Ashanda was asleep. She opened the door to Ashanda's room and watched her.

She still didn't know how this was going to work.

She went downstairs, took the coin from the table, went back up to her room, and opened her closet. She reached up to a hidden shelf, up to the heavy wooden box she kept there. She lifted it up, then carefully lowered it down to the floor. She opened the box. Inside was jewelry, rings, old coins, gold teeth. She added the coin to the pile and returned the box to its hiding place.

She turned out the light, reminded herself that morning would come, and went to bed.

CHAPTER FOUR

1

The boss forgave me, eventually. She always does. A year later, she gave me a job working at a jukebox in back of an old family pizzeria in Warrenville, Illinois, making sure that the music was a little more disturbing than it would be otherwise. When the pizzeria was closed, I could do what I wanted. I went to concerts, visited colleagues.

I even made a friend.

2

The entrance to the record store was a glass door covered with very old fliers- they'd been rained on, allowed to dry, and rained on again, more than once. Behind that door was a narrow hallway, partially blocked on one side by a pile of old issues of Illinois Entertainer and on the other by a gumball machine. At the end of the hallway was another door, and on the other side of the door was the front of the store, the cash register and shelves full of vintage video games and VHS tapes and unsorted piles of old electronics.

In back, divided from the rest by a row of blue plastic bargain bins and a fat concrete pillar, was Darius' kingdom. The pillar had a framed copy of the newspaper article on it, so that, as you approached, you might see Darius' face in black and white at about the same time that you heard his voice.

"It's not a real reflection of the music. It's not real, man. It's like a toy, it's just terrible."

Darius had worked in the store for nineteen years. He'd never purchased or owned a compact disc.

"Just thinking about it makes me mad, man. I just can't deal with that. They don't sound good! Why would you listen to something that don't sound good?"

Darius has an audience of two, father and son. The father is wearing a wrinkled black Blues Brothers suit, tempered for the office by a brown tie with stripes. The kid is in the neighborhood of twelve years old, thick red hair and coming up fast. He's giving Darius his full attention, a satellite dish pointed at the sky. They are surrounded by squares of color, submerged in light brown like fish in the ocean. The Pink Floyd pyramids. Herb Albert and the whip cream picture. Many guitars. Many stern looking women.

The only windows are in the back of the store, and they don't open, glass blocks level with the ground outside. Every time somebody takes a record out of a sleeve, particles of dust spill out that haven't seen freedom in years, or decades. Floating around, mixing together. It's a comfortable place to be a ghost.

"You listen to your dad, don't listen to your friends or the radio, none of that nonsense." He draws out the word, sliding in home on "sense", seventies cop-show cool. "You listen to your daddy. He knows the good stuff." Darius punches the man playfully in the shoulder. He does it wrong, hits a little too hard. The man forgives him, he's been forgiving him. He looks down again at his son. This is a shared experience- halfway between visiting the wise man on the mountain and going to a sideshow. Not one thing disguised as the other but both. Pity picks up where respect leaves off.

"For years now, your daddy always gets the good stuff. Wait a second, now I remember, I got it straight now. You were looking for this, right?"

Darius reaches for the shelf behind him, and it's only then that you realize how tall he is, how he's had to hunch to fit under the low ceiling. He unfolds like a praying mantis. "There you go, man."

Father and son go to the register, which is located on an elevated platform on the other side of the room that is not unlike a pulpit. Carl is behind the register. Carl owns the place. He takes care of the transaction with a minimum of eye contact. Father and son lock eyes for a moment as Carl wordlessly gives Dad his change, and again right before they leave. Son feels different, not quite comfortable. Dad lets him know that it's okay, that he's learned something about the world that he'll have to think about later. Son has grown up a little bit. Dad is proud of Son.

They leave. Carl and Darius stay.

"You working late tonight, Darius?" Carl sounds nervous and tired, as he habitually does.

"Yeah." Darius talks while moving, ducking down and hopping up again like a bird with a long neck.

A few other customers come in before the day is up, a pack just out of college, all dramatic facial hair and short sleeves. Darius puts on the show for them, and they leave with tall cardboard boxes. Closing time circles around. If you look directly at the front door and make an effort, you can see that the sun has set. Carl packs up. Darius doesn't even slow down. Carl puts his coat on and leaves. Darius keeps working. At around nine o'clock he carefully turns every speaker in the store towards the middle of the room. He vacuums the floor. He puts a turntable and a stack of records down where he vacuumed and turns the lights down low.

He lays down and stretches out, all six and a half feet of himself. He puts on a record and closes his eyes. He is completely still, right up until the first time Smokey tells us to take a good look at his face. He winces and sighs.

The song ends.

"Charlie, you here, man? Yeah, I know you're here."

He's right. I'm there. My voice sounds good through the old speakers.

"Here I am, yes it's me."

"Man, you had to do it." Darius curls up on the floor when he laughs, like he's doing half a sit-up. "You're the only one I'd let bring country music into my record store like that. You're the only one, dead man."

He's full of shit, he loves country music, he just does the old thing where if he likes it and it's not Johnny Cash he doesn't call it country music. I call him on it and that's an hour right there, the two of us digging into each other.

I don't know how he can tell when I'm around. Some people are good with children or animals or numbers. Others can tell when the dead are watching. It freaked him out at first, until I stared telling him about the time I saw Arthur Crudup play in '68 or the time James Brown visited the radio station where I used to be a disc jockey. From then on, he just wanted to talk.

He laughs a little too loud, repeats his jokes a little too often. When he's working he's learned to rein it in. He doesn't worry about that with me. If I were to be strictly honest, I'd have to admit that it does grate on me a little sometimes, but never very badly and never for very long. And he never suspects. I'm glad, I don't want any friction between him and me. Who else would I talk about music with?

The conversation dies down for a moment. He sighs, turns on his side, and takes the record off the turntable. He doesn't quite have the energy to put on the next one.

"I dreamed about her again last night."

Lacy was a girl he knew in high school.

"That's rough, Darius."

"I was looking at her Facebook. I know I shouldn't be doing that."

"Yeah, well. It's rough."

"You got that right." Darius puts on the next record from the pile, lets the needle float. I feel that moment, when it makes contact and the electricity hits. Like everything is coming down to the tip of that needle, but also like everything is rushing in from every direction.

"Listen to this, man. Just listen, I bet you haven't heard this one. I bet you haven't."

"All right, but I've got to go pretty soon."

"I know, Charlie. You don't gotta say goodbye when you go. Thanks for coming by, man."

"My pleasure." That part was true, in spite of everything. The part about leaving is a lie. I stay, hanging in the air, listening to the music until three o'clock in the morning, when he finally packs up and walks home.

I've followed him. He has a room in the basement of his sister's house. It's nice, but it's not his home. He'll be back here in less than six hours.

3

A ghost is a dead person with a job. When you're alive, you split your time. You work, you sleep. When you're dead, the line gets blurrier. You switch between one and the other quickly, or do both at once. You lose track of time a lot.

There are similarities. I still have a boss. I don't know much about her, I have no clear memory of ever meeting her for the first time. She has long brown hair.

A few days after my conversation with Darius, the boss calls a staff meeting. We meet in the Orange Room. The gang's all here. Neil from the laundromat. The bloody torso. The asshole with no skin that no one takes seriously. (The torso is literal, the asshole is figurative.) The little girl who never talks. Others. Somehow the table is as long as it needs to be to fit everyone and no longer.

The brunette is the last to arrive. She looks tired. She never looks tired. She glances to her side before she says anything. She's nervous. That's not right either.

The skinless asshole is sitting in the privileged place to her right.

He's wearing a tuxedo, his white collar stained by the blood and pus dripping down from his face. His name's Gary. He's got three names like all the bullshit serial killers have three names.

"We're going to make some changes," the boss says, and she sounds guilty.

She explains. I'm working for Gary now. Not just me. Lots of us.

4

Miles' Porgy and Bess is playing. I almost think that Darius is asleep when he suddenly speaks up, his eyes still closed. We haven't been talking up until now- I haven't been in the mood to share recent developments.

"Can I ask you something personal?"

"You can ask."

"You're not in the good place, are you? You're not with the angels."

"No, Darius. I'm with the musicians."

That gets the laugh I wanted, but it goes on for about twenty seconds longer than I'm comfortable with.

"Man, that's good. That's really good." He exhales deeply.

Lacy had gotten engaged. He knew this despite not having seen her in person since he was seventeen.

"That bastard, man. That bastard." He's talking about her fiance. He's a frequent customer at the store, but I've never quite had the pleasure, we have opposite schedules. In spite of the not-inconsiderable time Darius spends stewing about him, I know hardly anything about the guy. He was a year ahead of Darius in high school. He's very dark skinned and has baby blue eyes, which ends up being fuel for some of the nastier things Darius has to say when it's late and the devils on his back are acting up. He's a clothes horse. That's all I've got, really. If he ever did anything to Darius other than marry Lacy, Darius has never mentioned it.

"That bastard." No use talking to him when he's like this. I think about leaving but I don't. I listen to him talk. It's easier now that I'm dead, I don't have to keep track of the look on my face. All I have to do is keep my mouth shut.

The night comes to an end. I say something charming and he pulls out of his hole for long enough to laugh. He thanks me for listening and goes off to home, to bed, to sleep.

I don't sleep. I'm due at work in twenty minutes.

5

You don't talk about what you did. Why would you? You don't want to think about it, probably, and you're not often in a position to forget, probably. So if you have the chance, you seize it with both hands.

Unless you're Gary, in which case you absolutely will not shut the hell up about the ten young men you killed and ate in your basement in 1985. I'm in the back seat of his car and he's driving.

"Gacy can fuck himself. He was a clown. Gacy actually was a clown. In the short term, you're going to get people's attention that way, you'll get your little direct to DVD movies with your name on the box, but big picture? Nobody's impressed. That's not what I did. I didn't play dress up. I was a goddamn predator. I was an eater of souls."

"You haven't told me about my new job, Gary." I'm not trying to be rude. Now that the brunette has made the handoff, Gary has complete power over me. He can make my afterlife relatively pleasant, or he can go the other way. But he's not the kind that you can suck up to.

"You're going to like it, Charlie," Gary says. "Look out to our left." I look out the window. We're just off the Skyway southeast out of Chicago, I didn't see the sign but we could be in Indiana by now. Nothing ahead of us but highway. Strip club and adult bookstore billboards alternate with tall hand-painted black and white reminders that God Is Real and Hell Is Real. We pass an exit leading to a casino and the signs are briefly obsessed with it, only to make a return to sex and religion and discount fireworks as we go past.

"Right here," Gary says. There's an abandoned gas station on our right, an empty concrete shape barely casting a shadow with empty spaces where windows are supposed to be.

I blink, and it's like someone changed the channel. Lights, windows. Rows of snacks, walls of beverages. Everything but people.

I blink again, and the lights are off, the windows are gone.

"You'll be working there," Gary tells me. "It's a two part scam. We've got an appointment over at part two." He dabs the blood off his face with a white handkerchief.

We arrive a few minutes later- there are giant plaster nuts and bolts on either side of the heavy metal doors and a red neon silhouette of a woman's ass and upper leg hanging above them. Gary's still smiling. He has no lips to hide his stained teeth. We pull into the parking lot and another long black car pulls up next to us. Three men in identical gray power suits get out and slam the doors. Their faces are indistinct. The closer I look, the less I see.

"Get out, Charlie," Gary says, and I get out. We circle up between the two cars like high school kids.

"All right, all right." Like he thinks he's Sinatra now. "This is how we're going to do it. This is how it's going to go."

6

The next time I see Darius, I tell him everything. I can't help myself, it comes rushing out of me. And he listens. He's a little scared, anybody would be, but he doesn't huddle up and try to make it go away.

"They watch the casino, keep an eye out for guys that are having a bad night. The targets leave the casino, they're broke, they feel bad, they see a bunch of guys from a GQ cover rolling up to the strip club and they feel even worse, and then they go past the gas station, and when they see some place lit up and warm and empty, Gary's mojo kicks in and suddenly they really feel like getting a candy bar. Then they come in, and I'm behind the counter, and I make an offer."

Darius doesn't ask what the offer is. He's lying on the carpet in his usual spot, looking up at the ceiling. His arms are crossed over his stomach and his thumb is twitching nervously.

"The offer is that they can trade places with the guys going to the strip club. Just for a few hours. They can go get wasted and get a lap dance, and in return the guys that were gonna get the lap dance can do whatever they want with the target's body for the same amount of time."

"People do that? They take that deal?"

"Not as often as Gary seems to think they would. Gambling addicts mostly want to keep gambling, you know? I've had a few bites, but it's not the slam dunk he thinks it is."

"What does Gary do with their bodies?"

"I don't know. Nothing good. Part of the point is that once they switch back, they have to deal with the fallout of whatever happened. It's like it's their fault."

"If they let it happen, it is their fault. If you're the one talking them into, it it's your fault, Charlie."

I feel my little monkey lawyer jump inside my sternum, eager to come to my defense. I didn't pick the job, I didn't put Gary in charge, I didn't set up the scam. He snaps his fingers, he replaces me and I'm back in the bad place forever.

I've listened to the monkey many times. But tonight it feels small, and the rest of me feels big, and empty. Hollow. I don't say anything and the speakers are quiet.

Darius gets up slowly, his limbs long and straight and tangled. He stares at a copy of Little Criminals in a frame on the wall.

"I'm not making you up, am I Charlie?"

And I flee from the record store without another word.

7

It's midnight. I'm not due at the gas station until twelve thirty. I have time to think, to wander.

I'm out of time. Gary appears directly in front of me. I'm surprised he doesn't throw a puff of smoke in there, maybe a crash of thunder.

"You're late, Charlie." White silk, with a dark purple handkerchief sticking out of his breast pocket. "Time for work."

"I quit," I say.

"Are you fucking with me, Charlie?"

"I don't like the job."

He's still smiling. "Do you have any idea what I could..."

"Yeah."

And that pisses him off, and down and away I go, cast out of the world of men.

8

I'm going to spare you the details of this next part. If I just tell you what he did to me, it'll sound worse than it is. Let's say- and excuse me for being crude- that Gary drives a steel spike through my testicles with a hammer. It hurts. But it's not just the pain. Chop off my legs and I can't walk, cut out your eyes and you can't see. And you're afraid too, of what might happen next, of what else you might lose, of what kind of person you'll be when the pain stops.

I hurt too, but that's where it ends. I've already lost everything. I'm dead.

Gary does the best he can. He builds elaborate sets, crusty torture basements, the Spanish Inquisition, concentration camps, devils and pitchforks and iron maidens. For a while I play along and beg for mercy, but eventually I get bored and just let it happen.

The things he puts me through would shatter the mind of any mortal human being. But... well.

He builds me up and tears me down a hundred times before he changes his approach. He takes me back to the world- not all of me, just my eyes. I can see the inside of the record store. Darius is deep in the zone. His customer is a light-skinned teenager with wide shoulders. He's on the balls of his feet, jittery, a tough guy nervous that he might be doing something tough guys don't do.

"Anybody says Stevie Wonder ain't hard don't know what the hell they're talking about. The man was blind. All the shit he did, people would have already been impressed if he'd just learned to cross the street by himself and he goes and wins ten Grammys..."

No eye contact. He gives the kid space. I get a quick look at the stack. Darius isn't screwing around. Songs In The Key Of Life is kept company by America Eats Its Young and 1999. Emergency room medicine- get this kid in the air, stat.

Darius finishes and the kid looks down, nervous and angry about being nervous. Darius barely does anything. He lets the kid pick up the records, waits, and then, at just the right moment, he makes eye contact. The look on his face simultaneously projects perfect confidence and complete respect. Yes, these are for you. Yes, I'm someone who knows.

A second longer, and it'd be too much, but Darius disappears back into the inventory before it can go sour. The kid approaches the counter and pays for his records with a stack of wrinkled tens and fives and ones. Snow-shoveling, grass cutting money. He gets back seventy-five cents in change.

I get to see him leave, with a heavy backpack and a serious look on his face, a little more settled, a little more ready. And then I see Darius back in the store, now that nobody's watching, eyes closed, recovering, taking stock.

I'm proud of my friend. Then I remember who's holding the camera, and brace myself.

The door opens. Dark gray pin stripes, dark skin, blue eyes. No tie. He half-skips up the stairs like Gene Kelly, floats over to the register to give Carl a pound, and makes his big entrance into Darius' side of the store.

"My man! My man, my man."

Darius breaks his trance. A flash of something nasty and vulnerable pulses out in the moment it takes for him to get into character, but Lacy's fiance doesn't seem to notice. The two embrace. Darius is effusive.

"What's going on, brother?" Skidding into the last syllable, doing too much, but the man in the suit either forgives or doesn't notice. The two of them talk, standing close, smiling, congratulating.

"Of course you've got to DJ the wedding, man. Of course that's you. Who else would I even let do that? That's all you."

"That'll be a real job. I'll have to think about what I want to play."

"I can't wait."

They say their goodbyes. Lacy's fiance picks up his orders, pays for them and leaves with a skip in his step. They stay in character for as long as they're in the same building. The door slams shut and I see them both at once.

Lacy's fiance is still smiling. He's calmed down- he was putting on a little bit of a show, and Darius can be draining to be around. But he's happy. He was visiting a pal.

Darius is hunched over the bargain bin, his fingers pinching the plastic. He's staring at the door, his eyes are gun barrels. He stays like that, perfectly still, for so long that it becomes hard to believe, it starts to seem like an act. He grinds his teeth.

I want to smack him upside the head. He's alive. He can go for a walk in the park and feel the sun on his face, he can sled down a hill when it snows, he can eat a steak, he can kiss a pretty girl. And the only thing he can think to do is hate a man who came to visit him and share something precious, a man who was patient with him, a man who probably helped make sure he didn't get his ass kicked in high school, a man who loves him.

And suddenly I realize that I'm sitting in the Orange Room. The room is empty except for me and the skinless asshole. I'm sitting at the head of the long table. The record store is a visible in a flat rectangle hanging overhead like the view screen in a T.V space ship.

Gary laughs and slaps my shoulder, smearing it with blood.

"He's the next mark, Charlie. He's the one."

I pretend not to understand what he means.

"You and him," Gary says. "You switch places. You get a little vacation and we're back in business."

"No."

"Are you sure, Charlie?"

I don't say the word. I don't make the choice. But I want it. I want to be alive, for a day, for an hour, for five minutes. It's in me.

But I say no, again. I want it, but I say no.

But it doesn't matter what I say.

Something changes. My fingers are pinching blue plastic. I look up, stand up straight. At first I think the ceiling has dropped.

Across the room, Carl looks up, momentarily curious what Darius is up to, and looks back down, because who can ever tell.

9

The store's almost closed anyway. I tell Carl I'm leaving early. I step outside. The sun has just gone down. It was raining. Everything is cold and wet.

There's no use in complaining. I'm where I am. Darius is where he is. There's nothing I can do.

I walk down the road and when I come to the intersection there's a different fast food restaurant on each corner. Darius has fifty dollars in cash in his wallet. I order half the menu at each of the four restaurants, and just about as soon as I eat my last cheese fry I'm running to the bathroom to throw up. And even that feels ecstatic, wonderful, the pain, the acid taste in my mouth.

I go for a long walk along the side of the road. My feet start to hurt and that feels good too.

10

Eventually I'm pulled away and I'm myself again. I'm in a dark hole, half full of water. There's a long bloody gash across my stomach; rats and snakes are gnawing on my intestines.

The scene disappears. I'm standing outside the gas station. Gary's standing next to me.

"Your shift starts in five minutes," he says. And then he's gone.

I stand there waiting. I see the version of the store that the suckers see- there's a big white clock hanging above the cash register.

My time runs out and I take my place.

11

For me, the switch lasted a few hours. For him, who knows.

I wait for him outside and follow him back to his sister's house. I drift into the basement. His room is the size of a walk-in closet, longer than it is wide. He has a queen-sized bed, an improvised bookshelf, a pair of giant plastic containers full of neatly folded clothes. The walls are bare.

There's a tiny vintage seventies radio on the floor next to the bed.

His eyes open.

"I'm all right, Charlie." He's lying. I can see it in his face, the weeks of wondering if whatever took him will come back.

"I'm all right," he says again. "It was hard, but I'm okay. I'm tough. People don't know that about me."

He waits for an answer, but I just disappear. I haven't been back since.

12

I'm not the one who stands up. Not in life and not now. I take my cue and find my place and don't make waves. I didn't like Gary, but I wasn't likely to be the one to do anything about him.

It took a special set of circumstances, for something like that to take place. Here's what happened.

CHAPTER FIVE

1

In March, the sign hanging in the front window of the yellow house on the corner of Green and Fillmore said:

PSYCHIC
TAROT READINGS
SPIRIT CONTACT
NO APPOINTMENTS AFTER MIDNIGHT

In April, the sign said:

PSYCHIC
TAROT READINGS
SPIRIT CONTACT
SPECIAL APPOINTMENTS ONLY AFTER MIDNIGHT
NO SPECIAL APPOINTMENTS ON THURSDAY

The house had been abandoned for ten years before the Psychic Lady moved in. The elderly couple in the next house over were looking forward to having neighbors, and when they first saw the moving truck out front they did everything they could to introduce themselves. They knocked on the door, left cookies and letters. The cookies disappeared, but nobody ever came to the door. They only discovered the Psychic Lady's name was Betty when they got her electric bill delivered to them accidentally.

Years later, when Ashanda arrived, the neighbors only slowly realized that something had changed. They saw her leave for school every morning and come back home each afternoon, and after a while they decided that yes, it was the same girl, and yes, they were seeing her too often for her to be coming by to do yard work or something. And the sign changed, and a red bike materialized, chained to a tree by the side of the house, and the constant stream of pizza and Thai delivery to the house slowed down. Once they even thought they smelled barbecue.

The two of them thought about re-introducing themselves, but at that point they were a few years older than they'd been, and had had to worry about strange noises coming from the yellow house late at night that they didn't want to have to explain, and they weren't as friendly as they used to be. So they never did learn Ashanda's name.

2

At eleven o'clock on Thursday, Ashanda gave in, and admitted to herself that she didn't want anyone else to knock on the door after all. It was unforgivable for her to feel that way. It meant that she'd lost her hustle, Betty had made it clear that when you lost your hustle you didn't make any damn money.

Luckily Betty wasn't here. Thursday was Ashanda's night. She took Thursday because if you stayed open on Friday night you only got the drunks and Betty said it wasn't worth the trouble. Working on Thursday meant she only had to deal with one day of school short on sleep.

She was wearing a black dress, earrings, and very subtle makeup, faint enough to be smeared by even the slightest trace of sweat or activity, which was only one reason it was important that she sit on her ass the entire time she was open for business. People don't want to see you working, Betty said. They want you to be lazy and inspired and at peace. They want to feel like you come from a world where you don't have to get up in the morning if you don't want to. She called it the Jimmy Buffett effect. Ashanda didn't know who that was, but she got the idea.

Ashanda wanted sweatpants. She didn't feel like herself, wearing a dress. That too was the point. You shouldn't be yourself when you're working, Betty said. When you really got it you can stand in front of one of your regular customers in line at the supermarket for twenty minutes and they won't even recognize you, Betty said.

Betty had a lot of rules. But Betty wasn't Ashanda's boss, she'd made that very clear. Betty wanted a night off during the week, which meant the space was open, which meant Ashanda could use it. One share went to the house, the other two were all Ashanda's. Not a bad deal. Which meant that she was lazy if she didn't take advantage of it, if she put out the light and put on a thrift store T-shirt and spent the night watching black and white horror movies. If she didn't hustle.

It was a recent development in Ashanda's life to have someone willing to go to the trouble to manipulate her. She wasn't sure how she felt about it. Her feelings changed from day to day. They were on a downward swing right now, the two of them had had a knock-down sore-throat-from-screaming fight early this afternoon, but Ashanda wasn't going to make a decision now, when she was mad. When she made her move, she was going to do it with a level head.

There was a knock on the door, polite and gentle enough that the bells attached to the inside didn't ring. Ashanda was nervous for a moment- she really had thought she was off the hook, it was late for a normal walk-in and too early for a special appointment. There weren't supposed to be any special appointments tonight anyway.

She reached up to rub her eyes, remembered her makeup, took a cleansing breath. You didn't want to answer the door right away. The perfect time was after the second knock, right when the mark was reaching up for the third. Betty insisted you could hit the sweet spot every time if you worked at it.

In any case, the customer wasn't reaching for the door when Ashanda opened it; he was just standing there on the other side of the welcome mat. He was six inches taller than she was. He was wearing a black suit, white shirt, black tie, shiny black shoes, black hair thick and greased back. He had his coat off and over his left shoulder, like it was warm out, even though it wasn't.

Something about him seemed young; even though he was almost certainly years older than Ashanda, he came across as less than grown-up. The suit seemed like an affectation or a school uniform. He didn't walk, didn't move, didn't say anything. They looked silently at each other from either side of the doorway.

Betty said that you should never speak first, that you should never try to sell them anything. The mark would always talk. But time went by and the man in the suit didn't. He wasn't quite smirking; this was a power play, then. She decided, once and then a second time, to close the door and lock it and let the asshole walk home. She felt Betty standing behind her. A smart mark's better than a dumb one. They want to give you their money, it's why they showed up. Get their money. Get their money. Hustle hustle.

She couldn't ask him a question, couldn't hand him the steering wheel like that. She maintained eye contact. One thing getting locked up was good for, she could do this all day. It gave her time to think.

"You don't have an appointment," Ashanda said.

He shifted his weight to his other hip. "Sorry to hear that." Ashanda didn't know what to think about his accent- it sounded foreign, but only just, like he didn't want anyone to think he was too good at speaking English. "But you don't seem too busy."

"We have time for an introduction, if you like. If you want something special..." She hadn't planned on saying that, but was immediately pleased with herself, because yes, this guy wanted something special- "...we'll make an appointment for later."

"I think an introduction would be fine. Long as we're done by midnight, right?" He arched a thin black eyebrow and kept smiling.

Ashanda smiled right back. "That would be just fine." She opened the door the rest of the way and took a slow step to the side. He didn't move. "Come on in, please." And then he entered the house. She had another glimmer of worry, and reminded herself that it wasn't midnight yet.

She led him to the main room. Again, she'd been working on the timing. You didn't want to interrupt them when they actually moved to sit down, but you wanted to catch them when they were thinking about it. "My name is Ashanda."

"Johnny," the man said. They extended their hands and shook. She meant to do the gentle lady greet, to barely even touch, but he took her hand and squeezed hard, past the point of being firm. Trying to hurt her. She didn't break her smile, squeezed right back. When she'd been locked up, she'd learned how to do pushups on her knuckles. She was up to seventy-five every morning.

"My pleasure," he said. She only realized after he let go how cold his hands really were, colder than the weather outside.

"Have a seat," Ashanda said. He sat down and then so did she, not opposite him but next to him and around the corner of the table. He took off his hat.

"What have you come here to find?" she asked.

"Old friends," Johnny said. And then he started saying names, one after the other. All guys, all sounding like they came from old movies. Ashanda felt something tickling her brain. Old movies, black and white movies.

Gangster movies. The old ones. She'd never watched one all the way through. She'd mostly caught a few minutes here and there when she went to the classic movies station hoping for a good monster and was disappointed.

His skin was too pale, his hands were too cold. Of course. She interrupted him, was proud of herself for keeping her voice steady and professional.

"I'm sorry to interrupt, but it isn't midnight yet. And we don't do special appointments on Thursday."

Johnny stopped rattling off names. He gave Ashanda a look that was meant to scare her, but actually made her feel better. She dropped the act; Betty's voice disappeared from the back of her head. This was something else now.

Johnny saw that the hard stuff wasn't going to help. He went back to smiling.

"I was never much for rules. Story of my life, really." He took a quick look around the room, smirking at the scarves and the incense. There was a gaping red hole the size of a golf ball in the back of his head, in the same place where a bald spot might be. It was an exit wound. She didn't see an entrance to go with it. She thought about the way that it'd come up, and felt stupid for not figuring it out sooner. The gun had been in his mouth.

He looked back at Ashanda. "You kicking me out?"

"I can if I have to."

"Yeah, I heard. You've got it together, you and your sister." Her aunt, but Ashanda didn't correct him. "You don't want anybody getting rough all of the sudden. You don't have to worry about me. I don't get rough all of the sudden."

"What do you want?"

"I just want to know how my old friends are doing. I know that's an easier thing to do now than it's been before. Something to do with those glowing windows I see everywhere. I hear you're the kind of girl, if you say something will happen, it'll happen." He reached into his jacket, pulled out a neat stack of bills held together with a brass clip, and put it down on the exact center of the table. "Do you think you can help me out?"

Betty's voice came back. He was breaking the rules. You shouldn't let them break the rules. They broke the little rules now so they could break big rules later. But really, Betty's voice wasn't all that loud. And Ashanda was looking at a stack of twenties half an inch thick. She reached out and bent over the corner of the top bill. Another twenty.

"Wait until midnight next time," Ashanda said.

3

After Johnny left, Ashanda packed up the tarot cards and the candles and put everything in its right place in the drawer under the table, went upstairs, and changed into her pajamas. They were dark blue and soft. When she'd first come to live here they'd seemed like an unfathomable luxury. Like having a room with a door she could close. Just a few months later and she'd gotten used to it.

The money went into a sock, hidden at the bottom of a drawer. She'd find a permanent solution later. She decided that she wouldn't let herself count the money until she'd figured out a safe place to put it. That way she wouldn't get lazy and just leave it there.

Johnny had written down his names on a blank piece of printer paper with a red ball point pen. The list went with the money.

If Ashanda wasn't here, living with Betty, she'd be in a foster home someplace, or locked up. She'd been locked up last Christmas. A bunch of church people had come by and given all the girls homemade cookies. Only a couple of the really crazy kids said anything to their faces, but the moment they were gone there was a volcano of bitching. Gratitude was exhausting. It didn't matter who you were or what they'd done, eventually you got sick of it.

Betty was spending the night at Carol's that night, and wouldn't be back until late morning tomorrow, long after Ashanda had gone to school. They saw each other again that night. Betty was with a client. Ashanda locked up her bike and took the back screen door into the kitchen. She did her homework and got started on dinner. A good part of the money she'd made working Thursday nights had gone into cooking supplies. She listened to Betty work while she peeled potatoes. Something earth energy something something laughing at the client's joke Virgo something something. Crystals. Ashanda and Betty both hated crystals but people were specific sometimes, you had to know how to do it.

She put everything in the tall stew pot, turned on the heat, set the timer. By the time Betty was done dinner was ready. They both sat down. There was a little bit of small talk about Ashanda's English class, the silence. Ashanda prepared herself. Betty must have noticed, when Ashanda looked up Betty had already put her spoon down.

"I still want to go to college," Ashanda said.

Betty looked right at her, and Ashanda found that she couldn't look right back.

"Do you know how student loans are different then any other kind of loan that a person can have, Ashanda?"

"You told me this already."

"Student loans can't be forgiven. Student loans can't be dissolved through bankruptcy. You don't finish the degree, fuck you pay me, you finish the degree and find out nobody gives a shit anyway, fuck you pay me, you wind up paralyzed in an accident, fuck you pay me..."

Ashanda stood up. Betty kept talking.

"The whole point of learning a trade is so that you don't have to worry about goddamn vultures circling you for the rest of your life."

Ashanda pushed in her chair.

"I'll do the dishes later," she said.

She went upstairs.

4

They didn't talk about it again that weekend. When she went back to school, she took Johnny's list with her, and when she was done eating her lunch she went to the school library, grabbed a computer, and started looking up names on the internet. It got repetitive quickly. Every search led back to Chicago Crimelab or Mob Index or one of a few other sites like that. The librarian liked her and didn't mind if she printed more pages than she was supposed to.

She went over everything she'd printed up over the weekend. Almost everyone was dead, some of them for decades. A few were growing old in prison. One was a script consultant in California. Two were alive.

Johnny showed up again that Thursday, at eleven fifteen. She opened the front door to the house just as he stepped onto the porch.

"Midnight," she said, and closed the door again.

The bell rang an hour later and she let him in. She hadn't bothered to dress up. They sat down at the table.

"This is what I have."

The two who were still alive were both named Mike. Johnny nodded.

"Yeah, that makes sense. It's a little on the depressing side, but that checks out."

"Great. Pay up."

"Not yet. I need you to take a walk with me."

"That's not happening."

"You want to get paid, sweetheart?"

"I'm going to. Here, in the house."

Johnny reached into his jacket. He produced a stack about the size of the one he'd given her last week and threw it on the table.

"That's for the names."

He reached into his other jacket pocket and came up with another stack, a little smaller then the first. It took Ashanda a few seconds to notice that the bills were hundreds.

"No rough stuff. I promise. We'll be back before the sun comes up."

5

As they walked north, the sidewalks got nicer and more scarce, the houses got bigger, fences became red brick walls. Everything got quieter and darker.

"They live around here?" Ashanda asked. She had no idea what was or wasn't professional at this point.

"We all did. You know how you don't shit where you eat? This is where we ate. Even now, nobody breaks into a house around here. You break into the wrong house and whoopsy daisy..." He laughed.

They passed a house on the corner with three stories. It had white columns coming down on either side of the front doors and a turret bedroom like a castle from a fairy tale. Johnny stopped and stared at it.

"I wanted a place like this," he said, and Ashanda realized he was actually sad. He wasn't smiling. "I wanted a palace. I was never a car guy, I just wanted a big house. But everybody said I couldn't do it. We were supposed to blend in, nobody was supposed to get flashy and spoil it for everybody else."

He looked at the house for a moment longer, and then he kept walking.

They made their way to a smaller house with a red brick front, a house that fit the houses around it. There was a thick old tree across the street that cast a big, dark shadow. They stood under the tree and waited.

A van pulled up in front of the house. Two men in black ski masks got out and quickly moved towards the door. Johnny walked out from under the tree.

"Hey Mike."

They both turned around. The shorter of the two grabbed his chest. Johnny shook his head.

"Nah. You're not allowed to have a heart attack until I'm done with you." He smiled and did a twirl, showing off the bullet wound in back of his head. "Lovely night, don't you think? Take the masks off now."

They did, slowly, and Ashanda gasped. They were both at least sixty. No, Ashanda realized she was trying to have it make more sense than it did. They were way older then that. Their skin was thin and loose around their faces.

Johnny walked up to them. He didn't talk until his face was an inch away from one of the Mikes' faces.

"I still own you."

He switched Mikes.

"I'm always gonna own you."

He took a step back.

"You think you're gonna poke around, scare my wife, maybe find my safe? The cat's away? Right?"

They stood there, stiff, their mouths hanging open.

Johnny looked over his shoulder and winked. He looked back at the Mikes.

"Get in the van and leave, dumbasses."

They couldn't get back into the van fast enough. A minute later, they were gone.

There was a face in the window of the house. Johnny beckoned Ashanda to come over. She left the shadow of the tree.

"Tell me what you see."

She told him. A tiny old lady with big white hair, blue bathrobe, thick glasses.

"She's looking at you, isn't she? She's not looking at me."

Ashanda looked over at Johnny and saw that he wasn't looking at the right window. He couldn't see her either.

The little old lady disappeared back into the house.

"Come on," Johnny said. "She's probably going to call the cops."

6

They walked back down to Madison Street without talking. Johnny approached a bar and Ashanda followed him, not thinking about why now. There was an overweight man with kind eyes wearing a black apple cap, standing next to the stairs that led up to the front door of the bar. His eyes locked onto Ashanda even though Johnny was standing in front of her. He reached out for her ID. Johnny put some money in his hand, and he almost jumped when he noticed him. He let them both inside.

They sat down in back of the bar, in the corner opposite the dart boards. Johnny sat with his back to the wall.

"There's no use ordering anything. I can't taste it. You're welcome to have something, it's on me."

Ashanda shook her head. Johnny sighed.

"Are you going to be showing up any more?" Ashanda asked.

As he answered the question Ashanda realized that he'd gotten older since he'd walked into the bar. There were grey streaks in his hair, wrinkles around his eyes. He continued to get older as he talked. He shrunk, he hunched over.

"The only people who can see me are people I've paid. I don't know if you figured that out already. And my stake is gone.

"I really thought Anne was gonna be able to see me. That's how I always thought of her. Not in a bad way, but she never had any trouble spending my money, you know? That's why I married her. People told me she was too wild, but I wanted somebody around who knew how to have fun."

He took a look around the bar at nothing in particular. His eyes began to sink back into his head.

"They didn't need the goddamn money. They didn't even want it all that much. They just wanted to feel like men. What do they tell you about people like me in school? It wasn't all guns and bank robberies. We used to run things." He sounded like he was trying to remember something. Ashanda wasn't entirely sure that he was still talking to her. "We were important people, we talked to important people."

And then he wasn't there anymore.

7

She knew before she left the bar that she had to tell Betty everything that had happened. She spent the long walk back home figuring out how she was going to do that. Somehow she kept getting sidetracked into more college stuff. By the time she was a block away from the house she had it all organized, two separate topics all laid out like an essay. By the time she put a hand on her own front door, she had no idea what she was going to say.

She went to bed and skipped school the following morning. Betty came home around nine o'clock to find Ashanda sitting on the front porch with wet eyes.

Betty took Ashanda inside, made her tea, and refused to pay attention to anything Ashanda said until she'd calmed down. She didn't smile, didn't tell her that it was all right. She just waited, the way you'd wait at the DMV. After a while, Ashanda's eyes were dry and she could speak in complete sentences.

"I want to be able to tell people what I do and why I do it. I want to be able to point at something and say that was me. I don't mean any disrespect towards you, and I don't want to make it sound like I'm not grateful. I'm really, really grateful. I understand what you did for me. But this is about me. Not everything is, but this is. I want this."

Ashanda realized she'd been speaking directly to her empty mug. She looked up. Betty still wasn't smiling.

Betty got up, put her own tea cup in the sink, walked over to Ashanda, and put her hand on her shoulder.

"You sound suspiciously like an adult when you talk like that."

Betty squeezed Ashanda's shoulder gently, let go, and took her mug over to the sink to rinse it out.

"I'll give you a ride to school. You've probably got History class or something in the afternoon. God forbid you miss History class."

CHAPTER 6

I'm going to have to mix my metaphors, to explain this next part. I apologize in advance.

First, imagine it's raining. If it's raining a lot, maybe you're surprised by where it floods, but there are some places that flood all the time. Nobody planned it like that, it's just how the land lays.

Second. I already told you how being dead is like being asleep most of the time. Imagine you're a sleepwalker. You fluff your pillow, go to bed, fall asleep, and when you wake up you're standing in your kitchen staring at your fridge. You know where you are. This has happened before. But it's still a little confusing, it takes you a minute to get your bearings.

Last, and thank you for your patience, there's a bar. This isn't a metaphor: it's a real bar, down the street from one of the cemeteries in the town where Ashanda lived (although I hadn't met Ashanda yet at this point). It's not downtown, but it's not out in the middle of nowhere either. People drive past it every day on their way to the expressway, but they never stop. They never go inside. If they did- they wouldn't, it wouldn't occur to them, but if they did- there wouldn't be anyone inside to serve them. The bar is empty. Except.

I don't know how long it's been there, where it came from, why it's the way it is. It's just the place. When it rains, it's where the water goes.

I wake up, rub the dust from my eyes, and I'm sitting at a booth in back of the bar. The booth is full. Six ghosts, packed in like eggs in a half-dozen containers. Mostly people you don't know, but I know them. Colleagues. Some of them are just figuring out what happened, others are ahead of me.

Johnny is there, sitting across from me and to my left, his elbow against the wall. You know Johnny. Johnny's wide awake.

Torso is there too, but it's hard to tell if he knows what's going on or not. The girl who never speaks is sitting across from him.

Those of us who need to wait for the others, wait for the others. As soon as it's clear that everybody has their head on straight, we all start talking at the same time. We're all singing the same tune. Gary. Gary Gary Gary.

I'll spare you a transcript. Everybody was confused and had a lot of feelings they wanted to let loose, with the possible exception of Johnny, who didn't say anything at first. Conclusions were reached. Specifically: Gary was in charge now, nobody knew why, the brunette had disappeared, nobody knew why, nobody had ever heard of a time when the brunette had not been in charge, nobody knew how Gary of all people would be in a position to get one over on her. One last thing. Whatever transition was taking place that had the brunette stepping down and Gary stepping up, it was a work in progress. At least it seemed that way. Everybody had a story about Gary setting something up that hadn't been there before or trying to do something he wasn't sure he could do just yet. Added to that was the fact that we were all sitting here together, now, having this conversation, and Gary didn't seem to know about it.

Or we were wrong, and he was letting it happen, listening to every word we said. But nobody brought that up. Nobody had to. If Gary'd really taken all the way over, if he was what the brunette had been, then nothing we said or did made much difference. We were all his pets. And if that was true, it was worth it to pretend otherwise, to feel free, even if it was only for a few minutes longer.

"We have an opportunity," Johnny finally said.

"To do what?" asked Big Mike, Big Mike who'd been a contractor and built shitty houses and stole from people, and had done so for long enough and on enough of a scale that most murderers took the high ground when they spoke with him, myself included. "We don't even know how he made his play. What the fuck are we supposed to do? We don't even know what the fuck's going on."

"Tell them what you told me, Meredith," Johnny said.

Meredith only ever whispered, everybody knew that. Everybody got quiet so they could hear what she was saying. It took her a while to get started and even once she did, she would stop in the middle of every other sentence, and only start back up again once you thought that maybe she was finished.

"She took me to a graveyard... north of Mattoon, we rode the moon across the sky and rolled down into the cornfield. It had just rained..."

"The point, Meredith," Johnny said. She rolled her eyes and sighed dramatically.

"She had candles and cards and flowers and crystals and words that she wanted me to say. We went into the graveyard, past the odd fellows to a lonely little stone next to baby heaven, and put down the flowers and the candles and the cards and the crystals and made a circle and lit the candles. Then she said her words, and had me say mine, and there was lightning, and then she told me I had to wait outside the graveyard and told me to turn my back and close my eyes and not look no matter what happened."

Another pause, a long one this time. Torso was the one who finally lost patience and smacked himself on the side of the table. Meredith twitched, rolled her eyes again, and kept talking

"I didn't peek. I stood outside the gate. I heard her talking to someone. She was crying, then she was yelling. She seemed to be having a conversation, but I didn't hear anybody else talking, only her. When I did open my eyes, she was sitting on the ground outside the graveyard, just crying. When she got up, I saw she was bleeding out of the side of her mouth. She didn't say anything: she just called back the moon and we went home."

I didn't say anything, but my immediate thought was bullshit. I couldn't imagine the boss crying. I couldn't even imagine her sitting on dirt. The flip side was that I couldn't imagine Meredith lying either, or even getting the details right of a story that Johnny fed to her. She was telling the truth, or thought she was.

So maybe it had happened. Maybe. I was still rolling it under my tongue while Big Mike and Johnny argued. Big Mike had somehow gotten through eighty-five years of life without figuring out that yelling and banging on tables was not a shortcut to respect.

"What the fuck is this?" bloviated Big Mike. "What the fuck? This fucking... this isn't anything. This is fucking nothing."

"This is what we have," Johnny said. "That's what it is. I'm heartbroken if you don't like it. If you got more, please share. But it's not nothing. The boss got taken down a peg, which is not something you or I or anybody thought could ever happen. We don't know who or what or why, but something happened in that graveyard that blackened her eye. Maybe what's going on now is unrelated. But maybe it isn't."

Big Mike continued to blow air. "You aren't thinking straight. We have a new boss. That's all there is to it. We all have to get over it and we have to get used to it.

Like I said before, I don't like confrontation. What I do, when I have to stand in the way of where someone's walking, is pretend that I'm my father. Try to do it like he would and hope nobody notices the difference.

"Holy shit, Mike," I said. "I guess you're right. Think about what could happen if we actually tried to do something. We might be damned for all eternity. Oh wait."

What's funny is of course is that most of the time it doesn't turn out like anything my father would have said or done. But it did the trick anyway. Mike said something about how we were all fools, and by the time he got up he was already disappearing. Rain evaporating on a car windshield.

Meredith was bopping her head back and forth like she was on an old sock hop dance show. Johnny was looking right at me.

"Glad to hear you're interested."

"I didn't say that. Anything we can do to get out of having Gary eat our lunch from now until the end of time, I'm in favor of. But if you have something specific in mind, I don't see it. We have a lead, I guess. What are you suggesting that we do about it?"

"Two things. First thing," Johnny said. "We all have a little bit of juice, not a lot, each one of us. Not enough to be a

threat to... Gary now, the boss before. Just enough to break the rules enough to do whatever job we've been given, to come to earth and show our faces long enough to scare people, for you to do your radio thing. No big deal, separately. But what if a few of us got together and all spit into the bucket? What if we pooled our resources?"

"I'm not sure I see the point of all the 'what if'. We can't."

"I know a guy," Johnny said. "We're talking. Something might be arranged."

"All right. You said two things."

"Second thing," Johnny said. "Let's say we all chip in and put one of us in a position where we have some freedom to move around and investigate Meredith's story. They won't make it far enough by themselves. They'll need a partner. A face people can see, somebody flesh and blood."

"One of us. You're looking at me, Johnny."

"You're good with people. And a little bird told me that Gary kicked the shit out of you not that long ago. As far as he's concerned, you're a horse that's been broken in. If it comes to him trying to figure out who's moving against him, maybe he won't think of you right away."

"You've put some thought into this." Johnny smiled. I didn't like that. In life, I never met Johnny, but I'd heard of him through my father. Johnny was a professional. He could put a thing together that had a lot of moving parts. But he was not a nice man. "You're talking about a partner. A living person who could work with me and who'd want to. I'm assuming you have someone in mind."

"It just so happens I do." Still smiling. "You'll like her, Charlie. You'll get along."

CHAPTER 7

1

Ashanda's locker was near the school entrance, under the giant screen where they projected the schedule for the events that were happening after class that day, in between the two entrances to the theater, around the corner from the staircase that took Ashanda to the freshman Health class she had to take. Lining either side of the narrow basement hallway on the bottom of the stairs were display cases showing off what the pottery class or the mixed media AP art class was working on. When Ashanda left for the day, she made two right turns and took the sidewalk. Across the street was the football field, the nice one that varsity used, not the other football field that wasn't as good. In gym class they'd spent a whole unit skating on roller blades. There were giant crates of them in the gym office closet, sorted by size. Basically, Ashanda could not do anything or go anywhere in this school without running into something whose existence she would have denied two years ago.

She used the side hallways as much as she could because she had trouble with crowds, and she was happy to have a locker by the main entrance for the same reason. If she picked up her shit and left the building as soon as possible she could miss most of the circus. Out the door, two right turns, and she went west. The grass was green, the sky was blue, the sun shone in her eyes. Nobody got in her way except the girls track team, who blocked traffic as they crossed the street.

The area right around the school wasn't what Ashanda would have pictured before she'd come here. It wasn't a town, like a small town, and it wasn't a suburb, it wasn't just all houses going on forever in every direction. But it wasn't a real city either. It was a toy city. Not a little city trying to be a bigger one; it was happy to be what it was, like a little kid dressed up like a firefighter, all proud of himself.

She crossed the street and stayed on the sidewalk instead of following the path into the park. She didn't cut over until she was right next to the library. She walked through the big glass sliding doors and felt a little bit of the stress melt right off the top of her. It was three stories tall, and the first thing you saw when you walked in were the stairs leading up, lined by frosted glass that let in the sunlight. Movies and music and books and comfortable chairs. Ashanda loved the library.

She could lose hours here, if she let it happen, but that wasn't the plan for today. She had an appointment. She took the elevator to the third floor and found Dolores sitting with her eyes too close to a computer screen. Ashanda and Dolores had hated each other when they first met. It was Peterson's fault. Mrs. Peterson was the social worker assigned to whatever category of student they'd put Ashanda into when she'd arrived at the school, a group which also included Dolores. Peterson had put them in a group together, where they met with a few other kids once a week and took enthusiastic advantage of their right to remain silent. When she figured out that wasn't going to work she started pulling Ashanda out of class to say "Hey, how are you doing today" and "I hope you're adjusting to our school" and "You're a part of our family now", and finally, climactically, and several times in a row, "Have you thought about eating lunch with Dolores? You two have so much in common, it might be a good thing for both of you." Peterson was a machine.

The two of them avoided each other as much as they could, and when they were forced to be in the same place outside of group Dolores would just stare straight ahead, at the wall if there wasn't anything else. Things came to a head one day before Christmas break when none of the other kids in group came to school. It was just Peterson and Ashanda and Dolores in a room. Ashanda didn't say a word and neither did Dolores. Peterson just kept on throwing out one question after another, and each one would fall to the floor, and she'd wait, and she'd try not to look mad, and she'd ask another question, and Ashanda and Dolores would still not say anything.

Finally Peterson snapped. One of Ashanda and Dolores' favorite things to do when they were bored was recite the speech. "I just hope that you realize that there are people at this school who are working very hard for you and care about you so much and I hope you realize that when you the two of you grow older and develop a conscience you're going to look back at this time and you're going to wish with all your heart that you could go back in time but you won't be able to because..." This one all together, like the chorus of a song. "...time only goes forward, time doesn't go backwards, it only goes forward, so I hope the two of you realize..."

After that, Ashanda and Dolores became good friends. They didn't hang out outside of school, but they ate lunch together and when it turned out they had the same idea with college they decided to join forces. Ashanda only knew the broad outlines of Dolores story- some seriously bad shit had happened in whatever country her family was from, and she'd heard words like "hostage" and "refugee" and "asylum" get thrown around- but the practical consequences, the part Dolores would talk about, were that while her family might be broke they sure as hell weren't planning on staying that way, and that Dolores had some work to do.

Ashanda scooted her chair a little closer and scanned the list that Dolores had already dug up. She highlighted the scholarships she qualified for in pink. Dolores used blue.

"We need three rec letters. Nobody wants more than three, but we need at least that many." There was no just getting by for Dolores. If there was a single scholarship on the list that demanded three recommendations and not two, then she needed three.

"I guess we'll go talk to Peterson," Ashanda said.

"You can do that. I'll go second."

"Even after treating her like garbage all year long, she'd probably still do it."

"You'd have to cry. That's all. Please Mrs. Peterson. I've learned the errors of my ways. Please, please get me five hundred dollars off my tuition."

It was funny but Ashanda didn't laugh. Dolores had arrived at the school a year earlier than Ashanda and they'd put her in honors classes as soon as she came arrived. Ashanda didn't know how the decision had been made, but the math she was doing in class was easier than what she'd been doing by herself out of textbooks when she was locked up. It was an easy A, but it still said College Math on her transcript, not Trig or Linear Algebra or whatever else.

Ashanda gathered up her stuff and told Dolores goodnight. She went back downstairs, picked up her bike from the library rack- she had a prejudice that it was safer there than in front of the school- and rode home.

It was just starting to get dark by the time she made it back. The sign was lit. She walked around the side of the house, leaned her bike against the steps and went in through the back door. She could hear Betty talking to the client. She was so used to it at this point that she heard the music without paying attention to the words.

Ashanda started on dinner. This had been negotiated. The client couldn't hear or smell the food being prepared; it would be distracting, and it would make them seem too much like normal people who had to eat and sleep and go to the bathroom. Ashanda was allowed to get things out of the fridge and quietly chop up ingredients that weren't onions, but that was about it until the session was over.

Quesadillas tonight. The spinach was precut, so after she minced the garlic she had nothing to do but wait out the clock.

She started listening, eventually. It was impossible not to.

"Of course it's hard. I could tell her it's hard. I didn't have to, I knew that she knew. But I could."

The client spoke good but not perfect English. He took a moment to think before each thing he said. He had a faint but intractable Mexican accent. He was serious. Not mad, never raising his voice, not pushing anybody around. But you listened when he talked. Ashanda took a peek through the curtain, which she wasn't supposed to do. Big guy, almost too big for the chair he was sitting in. Work boots and jeans and a dark blue T-shirt that was meant to be a loose fit, but was still tight at his shoulders. Dark skin turned bright red by the sun.

Betty took his hands in hers. Ashanda took an embarrassed, silent step back away from the curtain.

"You can tell her now," Betty said. "She's always with you."

He breathed in, breathed out, and the sound was very quiet but encompassed the house, made the air feel flush.

"I know," he said. "But it feels like she's very far away."

"Close your eyes," Betty said.

He made another sound, Ashanda didn't know what to call it. Something halfway between a word and a breath. The room seemed to contract like a heart beating, and for the first time since the day she'd arrived here Ashanda fleetingly wondered if maybe there was something about her aunt that was less like what she said there was and more like what the clients believed.

The client spoke again, this time in Spanish. Ashanda recognized "hijo" and "inteligente" and "amor". He stopped talking. He listened to something only he could hear.

He shook, exhaled, muttered something under his breath. Ashanda peeked through the edge of the curtain again and saw the client look to the side, giving Ashanda her first look at his face. He was sweating, smiling.

Another random piece of advice from Betty bubbled to the surface- when you have to change gears, when you need the sorbet to clean their mouth out for the next course, make them laugh. This guy didn't need the cue, he was already laughing quietly to himself, recovering. But Betty wasn't letting him go. Her face was serious and frozen in place. Her God look, Betty called it.

The client took a minute to collect himself, and Betty let him catch up to her. He hit whatever mark he'd been waiting for, and picked up something from the table- Ashanda saw the blade of the knife peek around the outside of his body- and drew it across his palm. He held up his free hand and cut his palm and made a fist. Blood pulled itself loose and fell, three fat drops followed by a flood of smaller ones.

Betty stood up, still in character, and walked towards the kitchen. Ashanda was filled with a caught-doing-something-wrong feeling she hadn't thought she was capable of anymore and took three big steps straight backwards out of Betty's way. Betty blew through the curtain and entered the bathroom on the other side of the house. She emerged with cotton and gauze tape and went back through the curtain.

Ashanda heard Betty and the client talking softly to each other, laughing. He thanked her and Ashanda couldn't see it but the picture in her head was crystal clear: Betty bowing her head, looking back up, smiling at him warmly, a parting gift. Ashanda heard the door open and then shut.

Betty walked back into the kitchen, less imperiously than she had before. She was holding a black stone chalice in both hands. She rinsed it out in the sink and the water went momentarily red as it swirled down the drain.

"When I told you to stay away from the curtain, it wasn't a rough guideline, Ashanda." Ashanda waited for the consequence to drop, but it didn't happen. When she was tired, Betty was either unusually forgiving or the opposite, and apparently Ashanda had won the coin toss.

Ashanda made dinner and they ate.

"Francisco's quite a guy. Got married when he was seventeen and his son was six years old when his wife died. He doesn't have any family over here, he's done everything himself. I don't know when he sleeps."

Digging into the salad. "Why did he cut his hand?"

"It's how he pays for each session. A little bit of his soul. He can't afford to come here as much as he does, and he wouldn't accept charity. And it's good for him to think it's bad for him, if that makes any sense. "

"I didn't know that you gave charity."

"Not often."

"You like this guy?"

"Not in the way that you're suggesting and we will be changing the subject now."

Ashanda laughed, smiled, blood in the water, already knowing she was going to get shot down. "Is Carol gonna be jealous? Should I call her?"

"Little girl, are you trying to embarrass me? If you continue this line of conversation, I will call Carol myself, get Francisco back in here, and have the three of us re-enact the fall of Rome in the damn living room. Give the neighbors something legitimate to complain about for a change."

It was like getting punched in the stomach, Ashanda couldn't stop laughing.

Betty did the dishes. Ashanda helped her dry.

"You met with Dolores today?"

"Yeah."

"You find some places that will give you money?"

"We'll see."

Betty squeezed Ashanda's shoulder. "We will see." And that was all for tonight. Betty had another client in twenty minutes. Ashanda went upstairs.

One of the few things Ashanda had bought with her Thursday night money was an antique radio. It had been for sale at the Brown Elephant thrift shop, which was itself the best Saturday bike ride discovery Ashanda had made so far. It had cost her eighty dollars, which was way too much for Ashanda to just drop on a decoration that reminded her of the old black and white movies she liked, but she'd wanted it and she'd had the money and now it was hers. On screen, a radio like this one looked like a tombstone. In person, after some cleaning and a thick layer of furniture polish, it changed shape, became a living thing. Every morning she left it, and every afternoon when she came back it was still there.

She turned the dial left and right until something came into focus. Reception wasn't great up here but she got lucky sometimes.

"This is Charlie Harmer on WBLI classic radio, and this is Carol King..."

Ashanda hadn't heard this before and decided to give it a shot. She laid down on her bed, stretching her limbs to the four corners. Then she flipped over and reached for her backpack, and got out her homework.

2

The next morning, a boy in orange socks shouted at Ashanda as she arrived at school. It was crowded as people rushed through the doors and she didn't give him the satisfaction of stopping to look too close.

"So you don't want to talk to me now either, huh?" And then she was past him, and she could still hear him yelling but she couldn't make out the words anymore, even if she wanted to.

When she'd first shown up at the school it'd been more "Hey baby", like they really expected her to talk to them. When it finally soaked through that she really and truly wasn't going to be anybody's fucking girlfriend, out came the big guns. Turned out she was a bitch. Ashanda had half a mind to thank them for informing her. "I'm a bitch? Goodness, thank you for letting me know."

It wasn't a huge deal, as long as she just kept moving. And she had no reason to stay still.

Today, her little mission was to figure out where her recs were going to come from. She was coming up blank for options right now but hoped that if she went through each of her classes and thought about them one at a time she'd come up with something. She had gym first.

Tennis today. She took a look at the gym teacher to verify that he had not transformed overnight and ceased to be a steamroller with fat shoulders who'd never mastered the alphabet. After that was Health class, and after that was Consumer Ed, which was taught by Mr. Anatol. Anatol had a mustache that disturbed Ashanda, and had a big bald head that seemed as if it was ready to hatch. But he'd let Ashanda turn in her homework a day late once without losing any points for it, and make dumb jokes in class that he'd clearly made fifty times before but still got laughs, and didn't yell at people.

Maybe she could ask him. She put it in her back pocket.

Her last class of the day was math with Mrs. Gregory. She already knew she was going to ask Gregory for a rec, it was the only one Ashanda didn't have to think about. Aside from having an A in her class, Gregory had paired Ashanda with other students sometimes when they were having trouble with their work.

And there was something else about Mrs. Gregory, something Ashanda knew was there but couldn't name. Something that wouldn't matter, if she could just get the recommendation and keep going.

The bell rang, and Ashanda waited until the rest of the class had cleared out, which didn't take long at the end of eighth period. She got her stuff together and approached Mrs. Gregory's desk. She smelled cigarettes. Mrs. Gregory, and any place within ten feet of Mrs. Gregory, smelled like cigarettes, all day long, from the moment she came through the front doors until the moment she left. Smoking wasn't allowed on campus, and Ashanda had never seen Mrs. Gregory with a cigarette actually in her mouth.

The classroom was one of the weird old ones-amphitheater was the word Ashanda had heard used, a series of half circles dropping lower and lower like stairs as you got closer to the dry board. Ashanda waited one step above Mrs. Gregory, just where the cigarette smell became impossible to ignore. Mrs. Gregory was grading quizzes. Her arm and her wrist moved quickly and repetitively like a machine in a factory.

Ashanda was just about to speak up when Mrs. Gregory's pen stopped. It stayed where it was, pressed against the paper.

"Can I help you with something, Ashanda?" She sounded tired. Ashanda briefly considered apologizing and leaving and trying another time, but she'd come this far and it'd look worse if she backed off for no reason. She did it the way she'd thought about it. "I'm applying to college. Some of the scholarships I'm hoping to receive require a letter of recommendation. I was hoping you would be willing to write me one."

Some of the words would rattle in her stomach for weeks, would keep her up at night wondering how she could have been the one to say them. "Hoping to receive." "I was hoping you would be willing." Like she was at a boarding school or something.

It took a while for Mrs. Gregory to answer. She finished grading the page she was on, and only then looked up.

She took time to think before she said anything. At first, Ashanda thought she was thinking about whether or not she would give the recommendation. And then she just kept looking, with flat sleepy eyes, and Ashanda realized that she was trying to remember who Ashanda was.

"I'd be happy to write you a letter, Ashanda. Just leave me the forms, please." Ashanda heard a version of her own voice, or at least the voice she'd just used. Rehearsed, practiced, repeated many times before.

"Thank you," Ashanda said. "I'll bring you the forms tomorrow." Mrs. Gregory bowed her head in acknowledgment and went back to grading tests. Ashanda turned around and walked back up the stairs, feeling nothing at first. With each stair a little bit came back, like blood to a sleeping limb.

She usually enjoyed the walk to the library. It gave her an opportunity to think and enjoy being in the sun. She didn't feel the sun today, and she couldn't think.

Dolores was already in her usual spot. She'd been industrious even by her standards- she already had a notebook page full from top to bottom with highlighted bullet points. Pink and blue, pink and blue.

Ashanda sat down. She didn't realize that she was staring into space until she saw Dolores staring back at her, waiting.

Ashanda rubbed her eyes and stretched.

"Sorry. I'll get going."

Dolores didn't move. Her expression did not change.

Ashanda told her everything. Each time she thought she'd found a good place to stop and keep the rest secret, Dolores just kept staring.

"It's not enough to get a recommendation," Dolores finally said, when Ashanda was dry. "You need to stand out. She'll give you the same recommendation she gives anybody else who asks her for a recommendation. You need to find somebody else."

She went back to the computer.

Ashanda left half an hour later. She rode her bike home and thought. Something was still there and she wanted it gone by the time she walked through the door of the house. She didn't want to go to sleep feeling like this and still not knowing why.

It came to her as she waited for the traffic to let up so she could walk her bike across Harlem. It was the smell. Ashanda's mom smoked. She quit eventually, of all the things she could have quit, but Ashanda's earliest memories of her, all the Christmas mornings, all smelled like cigarettes.

If that wasn't everything, it would have to be close enough. Ashanda took an extra loop through the graveyard and went the long way around the block before she finally went home.

3

Ashanda hoped that there would be something happening at the house to distract her. She got her wish. She locked up her bike and came in through the back door. In the living room, where the main table they used for clients usually was, a man in a brown tweed jacket and unkempt white hair stood hunched over a machine, plugging and unplugging wires and then turning dials. The machine seemed to be made of brown plastic boxes stacked on top of each other. She'd have thought it was an old stereo set, but when she looked at each box one at a time.

The man in the brown jacket looked up at Ashanda for a moment as she walked in. At first he seemed nervous, and Ashanda's hand dropped to her pocket where her cell phone was.

She had the route already planned in her mind- run to the house across the street, call 911, run through the back yards if they weren't home. But he looked back down at his machine, and his face hadn't changed, and Ashanda realized that whoever this guy was, he always looked nervous. It was sculpted on top of his face like clay.

She took a step into the house and saw Betty leaning lazily against the inside of the doorway to the kitchen.

"Ashanda, meet Mr. Baker. Mr. Baker, this is my niece and business partner Ashanda. Mr. Baker is making some improvements to our security."

Ashanda took another look at Betty to make sure they were in non-bullshit-speaking-mode. "We don't have any security."

"Yes, well. Ashanda, Mr. Baker." Betty waited, but nothing happened. "Mr. Baker," she said again. Mr. Baker looked up at Betty, over to Ashanda, back to Betty, back to Ashanda.

"Yes, the, uh..." He tried to escape back to the machine and started adjusting knobs.

"Mr. Baker," Betty repeated. Mr. Baker popped right back up.

"Ley lines," he said, mash-potatoing his words together. "The energy field in the house is inculcated in reverse. I'm trying to correlate... the, uh..."

"Mr. Baker is setting it up so that we can kick ghosts out of the house if we need to."

He smiled, which seemed painful to him, and nodded his head furiously. "Yes. Push of a button, no problem. Just got to get all this stuff done first. Lots of stuff, lots to worry about."

"I hope you don't mind if we eat some dinner while you're finishing up." Mr. Baker didn't seem to hear her. Betty beckoned to Ashanda and they both went into the kitchen.

Betty spoke quietly once they were in the kitchen.

"He does good work, wouldn't be here if he didn't. And he's fine. He's a little nutty but he's fine."

Betty had ordered Chinese, which Ashanda might have taken personally on another night but was grateful for now. They were doing dishes when Mr. Baker poked his nose into the kitchen.

"All set. Everything's ready to go.

They convened in the living room. The equipment had all been stacked neatly and pushed against the wall. Mr. Baker produced two black plastic boxes, each one smaller than a television remote control but still a little too big to fit comfortably on a keychain.

"They look like beepers, so they won't stand out too much," Mr. Baker said, smiling a little, it was a touch that he was proud of. Ashanda didn't know what a beeper was but didn't say anything. Betty smiled and took both boxes.

"Thank you for everything, Mr. Baker. Always a pleasure. Are you doing your usual show this Saturday?"

That kept the smile going for a little longer. "Yeah, in the cafe. It's going to be really loud this time, I think. Even louder than usual."

"I hope to make it. But if I can't, I still hope it goes well."

"Thank you so much."

"Should I write you a check now?"

Mr. Baker frowned and Betty kept talking, covering herself.

"Please excuse me, that was careless on my part. I'll wire the money in a week?"

Relief passed through Mr. Baker's face, but the smile stayed gone. "Once you know it works. Have a good night. Nice meeting you, Ashanda."

Ashanda wasn't sure what to say or do, and ended up doing nothing, but as far as she could tell Mr. Baker didn't care or notice. He left the house, staring at his feet.

Betty put one of the boxes in Ashanda's hand.

"It's like a dog whistle. Worse than that, but the same kind of thing. Something dead needs to know you're not going to put up with any shit, press the button on the left. If you need to tell it a little harder press the button on the right. That's all you've got, though, so there's still going to be a lot of personality work involved."

"If this really works, why didn't you get one sooner?"

"It's expensive, so I didn't bother until now, but our unusual clients have been acting up lately. They were already worse than usual when you first came and you've seen it get worse."

"I'm just surprised that this is what works. That you didn't get a priest or... I don't know. A shaman. Whatever you get."

Betty squeezed Ashanda's shoulder and motioned her over to where the furniture was. They moved everything back, starting with the table.

"I did a lot of shopping and I kept an open mind, but mostly people in that line of work are either crazy or bigger crooks than we are. Even most of the people who do things Baker's way are high-functioning schizophrenics. Which would be fine, except their shit doesn't work either. Baker does what he says he does. We can't afford to worry about the style he does it in."

The furniture was moved. It was late by now, but Betty and Ashanda still had some time. They sat on the coach and drank tea and did some of their usual how-my-day-was stuff.

"You'll find somebody," Betty said. "Teachers like helping kids out, you'll find somebody."

Ashanda didn't say anything to that. She had to go up to her room and do her homework. She wrapped her arm around Betty's shoulder and squeezed, then went on up.

There wasn't much to do, math was too easy, but it took her longer than it should have. She listened to the radio.

"That was Little Richard on WBLI classic radio, thank you for listening to us tonight and we hope you're having a good time. Next on our station…"

4

Ashanda slept like a rock and woke up half an hour before her alarm, enough extra time for bacon and eggs. She made a big pile for herself and left some on the table for Betty. It was an overcast day, nice to ride her bike in and wake up to. She could feel the water hanging in the air but it didn't rain. She didn't think it was going to rain, she didn't worry about it raining, it didn't rain. She locked up her bike in front of the library and walked to school.

She made it through her first two classes and walked into Consumer Ed still feeling good. It was a lecture day and she spent the period contemplating Mr. Anatol's mustache.

The bell rang. The class went one way, she went another. Mr. Anatol was straightening the papers on his desk back out when Ashanda approached him and it took a moment for him to realize that she was there.

She hadn't planned on doing this right away, but she was in a good mood and felt the wind pushing her. "Would you recommend me for some scholarships?"

He blinked a lot.

"Sure, Ashanda. Yeah. I didn't know you were doing the college thing. Yeah, you're a good kid, I'd be happy to. Put the forms in my mailbox, I'll take care of it. You know where my mailbox is, right?"

Ashanda did. She thanked him one more time than she had to and he waved it off.

"People don't come to me much for that, that's why it took me a second. I'm happy to do it. Glad you asked me."

She left the classroom momentarily empty, happy, sailing.

Somebody stepped in front of her. She was looking towards the ground anyway, and saw orange socks. Two days in a row, orange socks. The boy was sing-songing her name but she wasn't listening very closely to what he was saying.

He was too close. She reminded herself that she wasn't locked up anymore, she didn't have to go crazy right away. She'd give him a second to back up, maybe yell at him.

He wasn't backing up. Still talking his bullshit. She was going to yell at him. She took a quick look over her shoulder before she just got started.

There was somebody standing right behind her, somebody big. She couldn't see his face, but orange socks had a friend that size, she'd seen them eating lunch together. Part of their pack. Orange Socks leaned in closer, still smiling, tilting his face towards her like he was going to kiss her, but she wasn't paying attention to his face, all she really saw was his hands, on either side while his friend blocked her path backwards.

"You're going to be late, you're going to be late..." Orange Socks said, and again she was empty, but it was a different empty. She brought her forehead down on the boy's nose and felt it break. Drops of blood on her skin. She turned around and saw that whoever had been there was gone now. People were shouting with happy voices, but they were all doing it from at least ten feet away. She turned back towards orange socks and yelled and cursed and kept yelling.

Gym teacher arms wrapped around her and pulled her away to an empty classroom. The bell rang. They took her to the dean's office as soon as the hallway cleared.

5

They had her repeat what happened a few times. She didn't try to lie.

Peterson made an appearance. Peterson was very disappointed. Peterson wanted to know what Ashanda possibly could have been thinking. Ashanda didn't talk to her. She sat in the chair until she was by herself.

Betty came to pick her up about an hour later. They were going to drive home, but Ashanda asked to be let out by the library so that she could get her bike.

"Fine," Betty said, the first thing she'd said to Ashanda that day.

Ashanda rode home. This wasn't good, but it was the first time she'd gotten in trouble. She'd get suspended. She wouldn't get expelled.

She came into the house through the back, walked through the kitchen, and found Betty sitting at the round table in the main room.

"I've got to go ahead and talk to Carol," Betty said. "You can meet with clients tonight." Ashanda'd actually forgotten that it was Thursday. "It'll be good practice. It's important to know how to keep your game face on when things have gone to shit."

"Why do you have to talk to Carol?"

"Where do you live, Ashanda?" Ashanda was about to answer, but Betty interrupted her. "You live with Carol, because Carol lives in the district for Oak Park River Forest, instead of living here, which is a good goddamn thing because if you lived here you'd have to bounce around at Proviso East."

Ashanda remembered Betty telling her about this when she enrolled, but at that point Ashanda had still been sure she was going to run away and hadn't been paying very close attention.

"So now I have to make sure that we all have our stories straight so that you don't kicked out of the damn school."

"They can't expel me for one thing. He came at me, he put his hands on me..."

"They don't have to expel you when you don't actually reside in the district. How hard do you think it would be for them to figure out where you've actually been living all year? All they need to do is want you gone, and with your talent for making friends it's not like you're going to have too many people sticking their necks out to...."

Remembering it later, that was as far as the conversation went. Presumably there were actual words involved once the screaming started, but for the most part they were lost in the fog almost immediately and Ashanda was happy to leave them there.

One thing- before Betty left and slammed the door, she said that this was her house and that Ashanda better not forget. Something like that.

She met with clients, feeling like shit, not sure if her voice was shaking, sure with each moment that something was going to go desperately wrong. But she saw everybody she was supposed to see and nothing bad happened. They all left happy customers. She hadn't thought she'd be able to do it.

She took stock up in her room, not sleeping, not knowing for sure if Betty had come back yet and not wanting to check. She almost went through the motions of packing a run-away bag, but she knew she was past that now. She wasn't going anywhere. She just had to sit here and feel like shit for a while.

She tried to think of everything she knew about Proviso East. She'd heard kids make fun of it as the ghetto school. Maybe they didn't have a pottery class.

She turned on her the radio, set the volume so it wasn't too loud, and scrolled through the frequencies from left to right. The red bar came comfortably to rest on WBLI and Aretha Franklin issued a stern warning as the music faded out and the DJ's voice came in.

"This is Charlie Harmer on WBLI classic radio and I hope that I don't have to tell you that was..."

Something clicked.

"This is the only station I have no problem getting up here," she said, out loud. "And this is the only place I ever hear it."

The DJ stopped talking the moment she interrupted, and when she was done, there was nothing but lukewarm static for a few seconds.

"You're not wrong about that, Ashanda," the voice on the radio finally said. "Not one bit."

CHAPTER 7

1

I'd been haunting Ashanda for a few days. I say haunting, because if I just say that I was watching her, it doesn't sound right. It'd be a tomato potato situation, but I am a ghost, this is the kind of thing I'm supposed to be doing. I see you, for the most part you don't see me.

And in Ashanda's case I had less choice than usual. We're going to have to back up for a minute. There was a second meeting at the bar a day later. More people this time, it was like the DMV at noon on Saturday, every seat taken. There were a few people I didn't know. A couple of burn victims. A guy in a Union army outfit with an impressive beard and the left side of his head blown off, standing in the corner.

Johnny stood on the bar and whistled.

"Good to see you all. This is not a small thing we're trying to do. If anybody wants out, now's the time. Door's over there."

Nobody moved. I'll say this for Gary's management style, he really brought people together as a team.

"All right then," Johnny said. "I'd like you to meet a close personal friend of mine. He'll be helping us with the mechanics of this situation."

Johnny unintentionally evoked Vanna White as he gestured towards the floor in front of the bar. His close personal friend appeared- didn't walk in, wasn't there before, but somehow was there now. Johnny's friend's clothes were bones, held together by strips of leather. Skulls around his neck, rows and rows of clacking fringe hanging from his waist like a kilt.

"We know the deal," Johnny said. "Breath in, breath out. Except for you, Charlie."

Ashanda's aunt's routine notwithstanding, blood is not the currency among my kind of people that you might think it is. Breath is what you want. In your last moments, you don't wish you could bleed more, you wish you could say more.

Everyone breathes in, everyone breathes out. The room is silent. Everybody's watching the naked man with the skull necklace. He's shaking. His hands start moving in little circles parallel to the floor, and his elbows are locked straight.

Then his body goes limp. He takes two long steps towards me. He punches me in the gut. That's what it feels like.

And then it feels like something else, worms with teeth chewing through me. I drop down to the floor, forgetting I don't have knees. Even considering what I've been through recently, it hurts a lot.

The naked man looks down at me with something resembling sympathy. Johnny is still addressing the crowd.

"You know the plans, ladies and germs. Let's all not screw this up."

Some of them walk out the door. Others just disappear. Soon the bar is empty except for me and Johnny and Johnny's friend.

"You get paid once it's over."

"That I will," says Johnny's friend. "Good luck, Charlie."

I won't embarrass myself by trying to place his accent. The bones around his waist click and rustle as he walks out the door, bringing my attention briefly and awkwardly to his ass before he's gone.

Johnny hops down from the bar and we both take seats across from each other at a booth. He explains the rules.

"As long as the spell works, you cease to be Gary's bitch. He doesn't have any power over you, and he doesn't know where you are, won't even be able to see you. He also won't know that you're protected until he actually stops and thinks about you. Which hopefully he won't do, because as far as he's concerned you're in pocket and he's got more important things to worry about."

I ask Johnny to clarify and he smiles like a jackal. He's proud of this part.

"Civil disobedience. Hippie shit. Really union shit, but I sold it different ways to different people. Everybody you just saw,

they're going to stop doing their jobs on cue. Gary's going to be running around putting out one fire at a time and it should be a while before he even thinks to check on good old Charlie."

"What happens when he does?"

"He'll start looking for you, but he won't know where you are and he won't be able to just snap his fingers to bring you to him. To get through your protection, he'll have to actually put his hands on your anchor. One touch, no more spell and you're back to square one."

"With a pissed off Gary."

"Yeah, that. So once he figures out that you're the one he's looking for, you better be ready to play fox and hound. There's one last wrinkle. Come with me."

We went around to the back of the bar. There was a poor excuse for an alley, really just half a parking lot that ran up against a fence that blocked off somebody's back yard. Near the back wall of the bar, in the shadow of the building where it couldn't possibly get much sun, was a dandelion, growing from a crack in the asphalt. Johnny pointed down at it like a stage magician and circled it carefully.

"You see that? That's you, buddy. That's your anchor to the world of the living now that you're out of Gary's hands. You've got a long leash you can walk in, anywhere in a radius of a few miles. Ashanda picks the flower, there's a switch and then she becomes the anchor instead. Nobody living will see the flower except her, although I guess we're all fucked if somebody runs it over with a car or something."

"What if Ashanda doesn't want to pick the flower?"

"You mean if you don't sell her? Then we're done. So sell her. We start the shenanigans at eleven o'clock tonight, Gary starts in on us, once he's done he'll probably take stock of who's where, he notices you're gone, he starts looking for you. I'll be generous and call it a three week head start."

And so there I was. Johnny wasn't a pep talk guy, pleasantries were short once he knew my questions were answered. My next stop was Ashanda.

I'm not what you'd call decisive. I avoid pressure. But once I'm in a spot, I actually rise to the occasion every once in a while. It makes me wonder sometimes, what I might have gotten done if I'd put myself in a spot a little more often.

Anyway. My first impulse was to find Ashanda as soon as I possibly could, and get her to pick the flower as soon as I could manage, and hit the road right away. But I thought about it. I knew what Gary had told me about her, and when I first went over to her house I gave myself a day to just hang out and get a sense of who she was.

It became clear to me, the way it does. Gary didn't pick the wrong guy, I'm good at this stuff. My realization, my magic window, is that if I come straight at Ashanda it isn't going to work. She's stretching her legs. She's comfortable, maybe for the first time in her life, and what I'm going to do is make her less comfortable. She's going to fight.

If I come to her, she's going to fight to keep me away. If I let her catch me, she's going to fight to hold me in place. So if I want time to make my pitch, I've got to let her catch me.

And besides, it really is a beautiful radio.

Thank you for your patience. All caught up now. I'm in a teenage girl's bedroom and she's upset.

"If you want an appointment, you can come back at the appropriate time, downstairs."

"I can do that, if that's what you want. But I'm not looking for an appointment, exactly. I want to make you an offer. I need something done."

"No."

Not a problem.

"I'm offering enough money to pay all of your tuition, finish off the mortgage on your aunt's house, and leave you with plenty left over. It won't be a simple job but the compensation reflects that."

She's looking straight at the radio, giving it her game face. Then she realizes that looking at the radio isn't quite the same thing as staring me down. She sits up straight and stares at the air in front of her nose, defending herself from every direction.

"Keep talking."

"I need somebody to go with me to..."

"Not about the job. The money."

Something is telling me that I should turn back now, but I ignore it. I'm too pleased with my little plan.

"I don't have exact numbers. But you know how it works. This isn't just me, I'm representing a coalition, and we all have a lot riding on this."

"Sounds like a great deal. What do you want me to do? Go with you somewhere?"

No more mixed feelings. I've made a mistake.

"All I have to do is come with you and you're going to take care of everything, right? All my problems."

"I'm making an offer. One professional to another, I..."

She reaches for the remote control and presses the first button. It hurts. Again, it hurts. Like a balloon inflating inside my skull and the balloon has electricity running through it. I'd thought I'd evolved past the point of worrying about pain all that much, but this has been a big week for me. I really don't want her to press the other button.

"I'll come back next week," I say.

"You're leaving now."

I don't actually leave, but I don't say anything. I keep a low profile. She listens close, and I can see her try to touch base with that little compass needle inside her that twitches when something's in the room that isn't supposed to be there.

She exhales. She thinks I'm gone. It wouldn't quite be right to say that she relaxes.

She lays down, throws the sheets on top of her, and tries to go to sleep. For the most part, she doesn't succeed. She spends the night thinking instead.

I know because I spend the night watching her. I'm not going anywhere. I need her.

2

She goes to school, just shows up like she owns the place. I don't think she even knows if she's been suspended or not, and she doesn't go to the trouble to ask. She gets through her school day the way that good kids do, half-asleep. She eats lunch with Dolores in the far corner of the cafeteria that nobody wants to sit at, the corner where the cheerleader cut her wrists open after school fifty some-odd years ago. Cheerleader's still there. She waves hello, I wave back, she smiles.

A woman with a strong family resemblance to Dolores is standing right behind her. Both of her ears have been cut off and one of her eyes is missing, with gouge marks around the socket. I nod my head, trying to show respect, but all I get back is intensity and silence. The cheerleader rolls her eyes. Lunch ends. Ashanda goes one way and Dolores goes another, her chaperone close behind her.

Math class wraps up, and Ashanda walks down the stairs of the auditorium toward Mrs. Gregory's desk. By the time she makes it to the bottom, the two of them are the only ones left in the room.

Aside from myself, of course. Gregory has her eye on me from the moment I walk in.

"You're dead," says Ashanda to Gregory.

Gregory sighs, and the veil is parted, allowing Ashanda to see Gregory the way I do, and the way she sees herself, her blackened cancer lungs bursting out of her chest cavity and inadequately concealed by her blouse.

"You're suspended," Gregory answers. "So I guess neither of us are supposed to be here. You'll get your recommendation, if that's what you're worried about."

"Everybody can see you. You collect worksheets."

Gregory glances in my direction.

"She can't hear me," I say. "She doesn't know I'm here."

"I have a job," Gregory says, to Ashanda. She doesn't give me away. If I had to guess, I'd say she was still considering it. "I have special privileges that let me do that job."

"Don't tell her I'm here. She's part of the plan to take out Gary. Even if he's the one who gave you the gig here, is that who you really want in charge?"

Ashanda: "What job could you possibly have?"

Gregory, mostly to Ashanda: "I don't like it that much, but it's better than the alternative."

"Is this why you blew me off yesterday?"

"I didn't blow you off. I told you I'd write you a recommendation. I will and it'll be a good one. I don't know why you got assigned to my class instead of something harder, but I appreciate your help in class."

"You can't think that things are just going to go ahead like normal now that I've figured this out."

"How did you figure it out?"

Ashanda didn't have an answer for that.

"Some people are people people. They draw others to them, they have a sense of what's going on. Bless your heart, Ashanda, but you're a dead people person." She risks a meaningful glance in my direction but doesn't stop talking. "I knew that the first day you walked into the room. It was like it used to be with the boys, when I was younger. Once you figured out which ones were going to fall for you, you had to keep them at a distance."

"I'm not falling for you."

"No sweetheart, but you did figure out that I was a ghost."

"So what's wrong with that?"

"Nothing. No one you try to tell will believe you. As long as you don't try to keep me from doing my job, we shouldn't have any problems." She didn't even look at me that time, but I still felt the cold wind blow. I wouldn't throw spitballs in her class.

Gregory went back to grading papers but Ashanda didn't leave.

"Do we have anything else to talk about, Ashanda?"

"Is there anything I can do for you?"

"You're going to have to be more specific."

"There must be something you want. Some little favor you can't do yourself."

"Why would you do that for me?"

"I don't want to get kicked out of school. Maybe your special privileges could help with that."

"I'm breaking the rules just by talking to you."

"If you don't want anything, then we don't have anything to talk about. If you do, there's no reason it can't stay between us."

Gregory put her pen down.

"I have the phone number for your aunt. I'll call tonight. We'll do our talking then. For now, leave the school. And don't push your luck by coming back tomorrow. Somebody'll take a second look at the attendance sheet eventually."

Ashanda left. I stayed behind.

"What are you up to, Charlie?"

"You have me at a disadvantage. Have we met?"

"I've met your reputation. What are you up to?"

"Just what I said. Me and some other people are taking down Gary and I need to talk her into helping us out."

"She's a child. Leave her alone."

"I don't know what Gary has you doing here, but I'd be surprised if you're in a position to take the high ground."

I'm happy to say that she doesn't have an answer for that.

"If you don't want to stick your nose out, fine. I've been honest with Ashanda, and I'm going to keep being honest." I'm actually not sure about that second one, but it sounds right. "Let her make her own decision."

She's still making up her mind. I've been given reason to doubt my instincts lately, but this time I go for it.

"I can tell that you like her. That's why you froze her out at first."

There it is, I feel it. She's still giving me a hard face, but the key's turned.

"If I feel that you're taking advantage of that girl in any way, I will tell Gary every word of this conversation."

Total professional. Replace Gary with "Mr. Henderson" or whoever the dean is and you'll get the right sound. I nod my head dutifully and follow Ashanda out.

I keep a polite distance at the library. Dolores' chaperone made her decision about me the moment she saw me and I have no reason to press the issue.

Ashanda gets a phone call that night. I get nice and close so I can hear.

Gregory: "I need a favor. Do it and I'll scare the hell out of the principal so everybody leaves you alone."

Ashanda: "Yeah, okay. What do you want?"

3

Ashanda waits until Betty's asleep and sneaks out of the house. She rides her bike north, but when she gets to where she'd turn right to go to school she turns left instead.

The curb disappears as she approaches the bridge crossing the river. Ashanda hugs the edge of the road. There's no traffic. She looks over the edge and I look with her. The trees lining the water are skinny and frail and easy to see right through, with one prominent exception, a half dead old oak with a thick branch curving precariously out over the water. Ashanda crosses the bridge and climbs down the slope to the riverbank.

There's a young man with a backpack. His silhouette is completely swallowed by the tree, so that Ashanda can't see him standing there until she gets closer. I see him a lot sooner than that, and swoop in to take a look at what he's carrying. There's nothing in there but rope.

He turns around and for a moment the two of them look blankly at each other like zoo animals.

"Let me buy you a sandwich," Ashanda says.

They start their conversation as they walk east and then north, and have gotten their introductions out of the way by the time they get to the shop. Submarine Tender is open until two o'clock in the morning. Ashanda and her new friend wait for their sandwiches next to a bank of waist-high vending machines that spit out plastic bubbles with stickers and bouncy balls in them.

I wait outside and watch them talk from the parking lot through the window. Ashanda listens more than she speaks, never tells him that it's all right or not as bad as he thinks it is. He goes all over the place- he starts out polite, gets mad, gets desperate, tries to get polite again, laughs at himself a little. She joins in when he laughs but otherwise he moves and she stays still.

Johnny wasn't kidding. She's good.

They exit the restaurant, she gives him a hug, and they leave in different directions. Ashanda rides home and I keep my distance.

She sneaks back up to her bedroom and calls Mrs. Gregory. They talk. Ashanda hangs up. It is just shy of one o'clock in the morning, but she doesn't go to sleep. She just sits in bed and stares at the wall.

She shifts. She's looking at the radio now. Each step, she stops and thinks about it. She crawls over to the radio. She rests her hand on top of the on switch. She turns the radio on.

"Who the fuck wants to kill himself because he got a C on a test?"

"Honors students. They're high strung."

"It's not funny."

"You're right, excuse me. The serious answer is that it wouldn't have the same effect on just anybody. He had a weak spot. Everyone does."

"Gregory had to do it. She says she has a boss. She says that's the guy you want my help going after."

"Right both times."

She thinks about it some more. She thinks real, real hard. I wait.

"You're still paying me."

"Generously. Hand to God."

I tell her where the flower is. I expect her to wait until tomorrow afternoon to go get it but she surprises me. She gets out of bed and puts her coat back on.

4

There is exactly one pay phone still in existence in the town of Forest Park, IL. It's by the Blue Line El stop and it largely goes unnoticed by the living. Picking up the headset is a little much for me, but I have an easier time with the speakerphone button. I call Johnny's number.

Somebody picks up.

"Johnny?"

"Johnny's indisposed," Gary says.

I do a quick little twirl. I don't see anybody.

"He likes to think he's a tough guy, but really? Give his wife one little heart attack and he starts spilling his guts. I'm glad it's you, Charlie. Don't let me catch you too soon. I've got plans. Once I'm done with what I'm going to do to you, I'm not going to know how to occupy my time, I'm not going to know how to top myself. I'm going to get all depressed when I'm done, so by all means draw this out, you sniveling little maggot, you run just as fast as you can..."

I do what the man says. I run so fast I forget I don't have lungs.

5

I make a single short pit stop and head to Ashanda's house right after. We weren't supposed to be leaving until the morning, and I was expecting to have to wake her up, but when I arrive Betty and Ashanda are sitting at the table in the living room. Betty's wearing a bathrobe and has a fat cup of tea steaming in front of her. Ashanda's fully dressed. She has a red duffel bag on the floor next to her that is just at the perfect point of being full but not overstuffed. She's either been practicing, done this a lot, or given it a lot of thought.

"No. It's not allowed. I forbid it." Betty leans back in her chair and waves her hands around. "Abra Cadabra." She falls forward again like a pendulum, puts her shoulders on the table, and rests her face in her hands. "Fuck."

"I don't know what that means."

"It means that I thought something like this might happen. I met you for the first time in a prison parking lot, it had crossed my mind that maybe this kid isn't going to do everything I want a hundred percent of the time."

"This isn't anything bad. This is a job."

"You're drinking all the goddamn lemonade if you think that's all it is."

"You think it's a bad idea."

"Yeah, and I know more than you, so guess what? It's a bad idea."

"So you're saying I can't do it."

"I'm saying that I understand with perfect clarity that you're going to do it no matter what I say. I appreciate you telling me about it instead of sneaking out in the middle of the night. And I'm telling you that you'll regret this."

I haven't had the chance to stretch my muscles since Ashanda picked the flower, but I need to get her attention, so no time like the present. I give the doorbell a poke. It rings, but it rings wrong, like it's in pain.

Ashanda jumps a little and looks over at the door, breaking her composure. Betty is completely still.

"Looks like your new friend wants to talk."

Ashanda moves towards the stairs, silently checks with Betty to see if it's all right, and has an awkward moment when she remembers she's being a rebel and doesn't care what other people think. Betty lets her out of it with a wave of her hand and Ashanda goes up to her bedroom.

She turns on the radio.

"We've got to leave right now."

"Okay. Why?"

"You know how I told you we had a bit of a head start on the guy we're trying to get rid of? It turns out we don't."

I expect... I don't know what I expect. Something more than what I get, which is nothing. A very directed nothing. She nods her head, tightens the screw. She goes back downstairs.

Out of something resembling respect, I let Betty and Ashanda finish their conversation in private. I wait by the front stoop. Twenty minutes later, Ashanda walks out. She's got her duffel bag in one hand and she's wearing a pair of cheap black plastic headphones around her neck. The wire leads down into her jacket pocket. I get close to get the feel of it. It's a radio, a big cheesy early nineties plastic box. Betty must have pulled it from the back of a closet.

Ashanda slides the headphones up over her ears.

"Good thinking," I say.

"You made it sound like we were in a hurry."

Gilbert Reynolds lived a block away from Betty and Ashanda, by himself in a little green house far from the street. He had a heart attack and died in his bedroom a couple of days ago. The bedroom door was closed when it happened and he left his front door unlocked. Ashanda has a pair of stretchy black winter gloves in her jacket pocket and puts them on unprompted before she goes into the house.

The car keys are on the kitchen counter, but Ashanda digs through the guy's filing cabinet and pulls out his registration and insurance bills and repair receipts and anything else that might indicate something was missing. I spare her the details, but even with the bedroom door closed the smell tells the whole story. She's a human being; she's not thrilled about this. It bothers me slightly less, if only because Gilbert is manifestly not in the building anymore. I take a look around his kitchen while Ashanda works. He has a calendar pinned to the bulletin board on his fridge; he volunteered at the Oak Park River Forest food pantry every Wednesday of the month except the first. On the wall next to a clock is a framed thank you letter from the National Association to Protect Children. I will not be hanging out with the likes of Mr. Reynolds anytime soon.

And he drove a white Corolla. I play lookout and she gets it out of the garage and down the street before anybody notices anything. She gets on 290 and heads east. Mattoon is three hours away if we can get clear of the city before rush hour.

Neither one of us say anything until downtown skyscrapers are in the rear view mirror. Ashanda asks me if it might have been a good idea for us to swing by Baker's place before we left, to see if he had anything laying around that might help us. Baker's place was my first stop after my phone call with Gary. The cops were already there, busy as ants with their crime scene. One guy thought it was a suicide, the other guy agreed that it looked kind of like that, but wondered why somebody trying to kill himself wouldn't pick a less painful way to do it.

I tell her everything. An early experiment with honesty, on the odd chance that she isn't taking this seriously. She gives nothing back, not for a long time. Not until we've long since run out of city.

CHAPTER 8

1

Ashanda didn't have a driver's license. It had been three years since she'd last driven a car, and even then it had never been for very long, never any longer than two hours, usually just to give Mike a chance to sleep.

Mike. Her boyfriend. Her man, as she'd said at the time. Three years older than her fourteen. The guy who drove the car and told her where they were going and how great it was going to be, and who led her to adventure and kept her safe, and who explained to her that it only made sense for her to hold onto the shit, since he was the one that might get searched. He was the one taking the chance, really. She shouldn't be selfish.

She'd thought about Mike every day for the first six months she'd been imprisoned. Imprisoned, not "locked up". Boyfriend, not "her man", although even boyfriend was a grinding compromise. Better if he just no longer existed.

There had been three Ashandas so far. The second one had come into being after the sight of herself in the mirror in a blue uniform no longer surprised her. The third Ashanda had come into being when Betty had come for her, and had still been in progress. Three was a nice round number. Four was not.

She thought about pulling over the car, wiping her fingerprints, and walking north until she found an El stop that would take her back home. But she didn't. She kept going.

On the sunny side, she did enjoy highway driving. And it'd been a really long time.

The sun was up, the road was mostly empty. For a while, Ashanda let herself forget that she wasn't alone. She decided that would be a bad habit to get into. She turned on the radio.

"We have a few things we've got to talk about."

"I'm all ears," Charlie said.

"I've only ever really talked to..."

"To a ghost."

"I've only ever talked to a ghost a few times, only when I was working. I've never been able to ask questions. I don't know what the rules are."

"There might not be as many rules as you'd think. But ask away."

"Explain to me what you just said, please."

A moment's pause, he had to think about it. "I guess what I mean is that I might not know as much as you think. We don't have much in common all the time."

"Tell me what they do have in common, then."

Fatigue was getting to her now, she hadn't slept. She wanted a fight, but the voice coming through the speakers didn't give it to her.

"Well, night time is the best time for doing anything strenuous. Everything gets harder when the sun comes up. And generally, the more you dish out, the more you can take."

"You're going to have to explain that too."

"If you have a body, then you can be hurt. Maybe not die exactly, that ship's sailed, but you can be disabled."

"Baker's box hurt you and you don't have a body."

"It did. That was a new one for me. But there's lots of things like that. Surprises. Rules you can count on are hard to come by."

"So if your boss has a skeleton try to strangle me I should hope I get surprised." Ashanda put all the weight on 'your boss'. Still pushing for it.

"If my boss..." He didn't do what Ashanda did but didn't go light either, it was like he'd read what she'd said on a piece of paper and written her a letter back. "...pins down where we are and what we're doing, we're probably finished no matter what happens."

Nowhere to go from there, so she went nowhere. She was not going to let him be reasonable. She drove for a while, silently.

"I've thought of another rule," Charlie said.

Ashanda kept her eyes on the road.

"No one who lived a good life comes back. Whatever they're up to, they don't bother the living. Every so often, you run into somebody who says they're back for revenge like in the movies, or that they're just hanging around to make sure their kids are all right. It's crap. Maybe they decide to do those things as long as they're around, but that's not what makes them what they are. Ghosts are mistakes that won't stop explaining themselves."

"And that's you too."

"Very much so."

"So what did you do?" She thought she was throwing another punch, but the anger disappeared by the time the words made it out of her mouth. The red ball in a magic trick, out of sight.

"I'm not going to tell you. I'm ashamed."

More driving.

"Another thing, personal to me. I'm used to just hanging out and watching people. You don't have to talk to me if you don't want to. It's not rude or anything. I'll be around if you need me, but I don't need entertaining."

Not hostile. Like he was an unexpected guest in her home.

She took him at his word, tried to figure out how she felt about this. She put on DCI and had to decide on the volume. She did not want attention; she was driving a stolen car. She didn't want to fall asleep either. She tried to find a compromise. She wished she could just turn it all the way up.

2

For a long time, there were walls lining the highway with bushes and tree branches flowing over the top of them, and Ashanda could imagine jungles on the other side. Eventually the walls disappeared, replaced by farms, rolling green hills as far as Ashanda could see. At around the same time the static started beating out the music and Ashanda turned the volume down.

She passed a set of three white signs.

SOMETHING TO PONDER.

AN ARMED CITIZEN.

AS FIRST RESPONDER.

She passed a blue water tower. "Gilman, the City of Crossroads."

The highway straightened out. She kept the wheel steady with one hand and rested the other on her knee.

She entered Coles County.

She was fifteen miles away from Mattoon. She caught herself drifting into the right shoulder. The second time the rumble strips woke her up.

"It might not be a bad idea to get some rest," Charlie said. "There might be someone waiting for us by the cemetery or in town, but probably not this far out."

"I'm not going to sleep in the car."

"There's some money in an envelope in the glove compartment. Not a lot, we'll have to figure for when it runs out, but you can get a cheap room."

More memories of Michael. Motel 6's were the cheap ones, cheaper the further from the city you got. Ashanda got lucky and found one a mile down the road.

She registered under the name Betty Davis. The man at the counter looked at her more than twice over thick plastic glasses. She put five twenties on the counter when he asked for some ID. He looked at her like he was terribly offended and then took the money.

The room smelled like wet dust. Ashanda told herself she was going to binge on cable before she went to sleep, but as soon as she laid down she was out cold. When she woke up again, it was not quite five o'clock in the morning and still dark. No continental breakfast for two hours, and she didn't know when the cemetery was going to open.

She slides her headphones down over her ears.

"Is my aunt going to be okay?"

She tried to make it sound casual, but it still wasn't that long a drive back home. If the ghost tried to reassure her, she was out of here.

"She seems like she can handle herself," the voice in her ears said. "But I don't know. The sooner we wrap this up, the better."

Something settled. Ashanda sat down in the recliner next to the bed. She stretched her hands towards the ceiling and her feet towards the TV, and yawned as hard as she could.

"Breakfast first."

"You got it," Charlie said.

3

Ashanda took a shower, changed clothes, repacked, left a good tip for the cleaning lady, left the room, and declared war on the continental breakfast bar. Many bowls of granola and stale donuts later, she grabbed an entire bunch of bananas and walked out.

The cemetery was right up against downtown Mattoon, a right turn from the Burger King, which was a flat squat red building with a modest sign out in front of it, white lights against black letters. Ashanda wasn't sure it was a real Burger King. She wasn't sure it was a real town. She'd never seen real white picket fences before. It looked like the beginning part of a Twilight Zone episode, the part that was meant to show that everything was normal. At the same time, she could tell people lived here. There was traffic. Windows had fliers in them. Some stores were boarded up and others were shiny and new. This was a real place, a whole world that had never crossed her mind.

She made a quick stop at a convenience store after she parked the car to buy an umbrella and a large bag of M&M's. There were four guys ahead of her in the check-out line. Three of them were wearing Marines T-shirts and the fourth looked nervous.

The entrance was two brick columns with a fifteen-foot tall iron arc spanning between them like a rainbow and the words Dodge Grove Cemetery spelled in iron. Behind it was a mighty flagpole, the tallest object of any kind in sight. There was only a gentle breeze, but somehow that was enough to make the flag wave. There was no traffic and Ashanda walked down the middle of the road, right towards the flagpole, like she was being dragged there by a magnet.

An elderly man in a wifebeater was sitting on a lawn chair on the front porch of one of the last houses before the gate. He was leaning back, very nearly dead, until Ashanda came by. He stared at her, turning his head to track her as she walked by. In a genuine moment of optimism, Ashanda smiled at him and said hello. He just kept staring.

She exhaled as she passed through the cemetery gate, tried to let it go by. She took a look around before she started talking to Charlie. She didn't want to look like a crazy person.

"Odd fellows and baby heaven. That's all we have?"

"I'm sorry to say that's it. I guess we're going to have to look around."

Ashanda did one big loop around the walking path that covered most of the middle part of the cemetery, then did another long walk back the way she'd came. Then she did a big circle around the outside edge. Aside from the front gate, there were no walls or fences around the edge, just a point where it stopped and the cornfields started.

Looking quickly over each stone, she saw the same poem repeated half a dozen times.

IF TEARS COULD BUILD A STAIRWAY,
AND MEMORIES A LANE,
I'D WALK RIGHT UP TO HEAVEN
AND BRING YOU HOME AGAIN

She saw a Nascar racer, carved into black marble with a laser.

She saw a white patent leather high-heeled shoe leaning against a grave, full of orange flowers.

"Ashanda." Charlie. "Turn around and take a look at those flags."

She did. She saw three flagpoles, each one about half as tall as the main flag pole by the entrance. They were all clustered around a black monument.

ODD FELLOWS

There was a symbol engraved under the words, a chain with three links, pulled tight.

Ashanda stood next to the monument and turned around in a circle. There eight rows of tombstones arranged in circles getting further and further away from the flags, like a dartboard.

Ashanda stopped. Some of the paths through the cemetery had been marked with little street signs on metal poles. Not all of them, but some. The one near the entrance was marked as Western Front Drive.

There was another little street sign, right outside the furthest circle. It was white and the words written on it seemed to be written in black marker.

"Baby Heaven Sec.-8"

Ashanda walked towards Baby Heaven, steering around Odd Fellows' tombstones. At the halfway point, she looked down. Most of the stones were grouped together by family. One wasn't. An old one, soft stone, worn away by time.

ETHAN PALE
ANGEL'S VOICE
DEVIL'S FINGERS
? - 1948

"Guitar player, maybe," Charlie said.

"I guess." Ashanda had to think about it. Guitar player, fingers? She supposed that was what you played guitar with. Still a weird thing to talk about the devil on a tombstone.

She took a sheet of blank white printer paper and a pencil out of her back pocket. She pressed the paper to the tombstone and rubbed the side of the pencil lead against it.

In her headphones: "You bring that with you everywhere?"

"If I know I'm going to a cemetery, sure."

Charlie laughed. "Dead people person."

Ashanda brought back the last time she'd heard that, noted that she hadn't known Charlie was listening, and kept her poker face on the whole time. She folded up her paper, put it in her back pocket, took out her phone, and took a picture of the tombstone just to be on the safe side.

She left the cemetery. The old man in the lawn chair came back to life as she went by. She waved goodbye. She thought about skipping all the way back to her car, but decided that would be going too far. If the bumper stickers around here meant anything, there was a good chance he was armed.

Ashanda was hungry. She went to Burger King. There was a newspaper flier attached to the wall with the whole story. This place had the name before the other Burger King. You couldn't buy a Whopper anywhere in twenty miles of Mattoon, IL. Ashanda got a burger and a shake and waited until the teenager at the front counter started mopping the floor of the kitchen before she started talking to Charlie.

"So we have a name and we think maybe he was a guitar player. And he's important, but we have no idea why."

"It's more than we had this morning."

"That wasn't a charity cemetery."

"I'm not sure what you mean."

"Back home, they gave cheap cemetery plots free to poor people sometimes. If you walked around, you'd see little patches with cheap tombstones. But all the stones we were just looking at were family plots that people paid for, and somebody put down a little extra so that Ethan Pale could get a special inscription."

"So we find out who paid for the stone and maybe that tells us who Ethan Pale is. Nice work, detective."

"Not yet. I still don't know how we figure out who paid for the stone."

"There's a historical society. They'd at least know where to look. You could hit them up tomorrow morning."

Ashanda finished her shake. She carried the empty cup lightly in her hand. A boy her age came by with a mop and Ashanda waited until he was gone.

"Where am I gonna sleep tonight, Charlie?"

"Will you be okay camping out in the car?"

"The police will drive by and see the little brown girl sleeping in a dead man's car."

"I can go look around."

"Take your time. I'm getting fries."

Charlie was back in her ear ten minutes later, pleased with himself. The place he'd found was in walking distance, not far from the path she'd traced to get to the cemetery, just one more right turn. The street had been busier once. The right side had a few storefronts open, a used bookstore and an antique shop and an art gallery mostly devoted to landscapes. The left side was dominated by an old movie theater. TIME in big white letters, climbing towards the sky against red and yellow stripes, and a clock hanging over the box office, trapped at two minutes after five.

Charlie was lookout. One of the boards covering one of the front windows was barely even nailed on. Getting it back in place once she'd gotten inside the theater was harder than yanking it off in the first place. She got out her phone and waved the light in front of her.

Thick red carpeting, buried under dust that also floated in the air. Gold paint, patterns in the trim that followed where the wall met the ceiling. Everything smelled like animal shit. She opened the door to the theater and she heard things scurrying away between the seats. The screen was still there, four perfect corners. Comedy and tragedy were looking down from the balcony on the left and a lion with angel's wings was hovering on the right. She imagined the curtains opening, the audience going silent, like in church. Dracula and the Bride of Frankenstein.

Ashanda climbed through the hole into the booth. No projector, no nothing. She'd held out hope for hidden treasures, rolls of film or old posters, anything, but there was nothing, just four bare walls.

She dropped her duffle bag and laid down on the carpet, using it as a pillow.

"It's a little early to go to sleep," Charlie said to her headphones.

"It doesn't feel like it, but you're right. I'm just making sure I'll fit. Do we have anything else to do around here?"

"Nothing I can think of. Do you want to call your aunt?"

"We decided that I shouldn't. Our story if anybody comes asking around is that I got mad because of the thing at school and ran away." She sighed, closed her eyes, stretched her legs. "Nobody's going to be too surprised to hear that. Is there anything dead around here that we have to worry about?"

"No, I haven't seen a single ghost since we got to town."

"That's good?"

"It's a little strange. I was worried Gary might have somebody keeping an eye out for us."

"But there was nobody at all. Is that weird?"

"Yeah, it is. Especially with the graveyard right there."

She sat up. "So what does it mean?"

"I don't know."

She rolled her eyes and laid back down. "Great. I'm going to hang out here until I get hungry. Can you keep an eye out please and tell me if anything's going on?"

"Maybe I should go for a stroll around the block and see if I notice anything."

"That'd be good. Keep an eye out for a grocery store too."

"You got it. I'll be back in a bit."

"All right."

The voice in her headphones went quiet. Ashanda wondered if he was gone. For all she knew, he hadn't gone anywhere. He could be watching her right now.

She propped herself up on her elbow and dug into her bag. She was glad she brought a book.

CHAPTER 9

1

I've never tried to hide from another ghost before. If I want to talk to someone, I seek them out. If I don't, I stay away, and that's about all. I can tell myself I'm keeping a low profile, but if I'm being honest with myself I know that doesn't mean too much.

If Johnny wasn't telling stories, then Gary himself cannot see me. Everybody else is everybody else. I can stay still and risk not seeing anyone who might be coming, or I can hop around and risk them seeing me.

I make my choice and do another sweep. I notice something that I missed before. A half a mile away from the movie theater, there's a pair of athletic fields, tennis and volleyball and baseball on one side of the street and a big all-American football field on the other. The fences surrounding both halves are covered in signs for local businesses.

On the football field, invisible to the mortal eye, is a young man in a badly dated football uniform, tirelessly kicking one field goal after another. I watch him from a great distance. He doesn't appear to see me.

I look around some more. No more dead people, but there is a grocery store a short drive away that closes at ten o'clock. I let Ashanda know so she can go get something to eat before the sun goes down. She duct tapes over the bolt by the back door of the theater so she can get back in and drives to the grocery store, where she breaks her last twenty dollar bill to buy some hummus, a bag of carrot sticks, and box of granola bars. She eats her dinner at a picnic table and she goes back to the theater.

She gets settled, reads fifty more pages of The Joy Luck Club and falls asleep. I watch her. For an hour, I do that.

I'm bored.

I head up to the roof of the theater and look around. I don't see anything I hadn't seen before. It's darker than I'm used to, easier to see the stars. Everyone sleeping the sleep of the just, except for a dead teenager doing wind sprints.

There are pros and cons to introducing myself. It might be a good idea to know why there aren't any other ghosts around, and maybe he knows why. Maybe asking him is worth the risk of someone knowing I'm here and maybe it isn't. But the reason I do it is because the alternative is sitting in a dark, silent room for eight hours.

The football player stands and waits as I get closer.

"You're the guy Gary has everybody looking for," the football player says.

My stomach does a backflip. "Does that include you?" I try not to sound like I care too much.

"No. I don't like Gary. He kept saying that if I was the one who spotted you, he'd set me up with a nice car and naked cheerleaders and shit. I kept telling him that I'm gay and he wouldn't believe me."

He talks like he doesn't even know what lying was. He could have played a cowboy in an old movie. I feel sorry for the girls back in the day.

"Do I have to worry about anybody else looking for me?"

"I don't think so, not around here. Gary rounded up the guys at the cemetery who died in the riot and took them somewhere. I don't know where they went."

"Gary was here?"

"A couple of days ago."

Gary already got to Johnny. He knows about me. He almost certainly knows about Ashanda. The car was my idea. Even if Gary thought to canvass the neighborhood, I don't know if he'd have the brains to track down a license plate. I do know, actually, Gary's a moron, but a lot depends on if he can control his ego long enough to recruit people smarter than he is.

I talk to the football player for just a little while longer. He was usually sleeping with somebody, from the glory days on through the beer gut and disability years, and he'd always done everything he could to make the guy feel like shit. He didn't apologize; he obviously wasn't proud, but he just said what happened. I was worried for a moment that he was going to turn it back on me and ask for my story but he didn't pry, which I appreciated more but left the conversation with nowhere to go.

I headed back to the theater. I still had a few hours to go until morning. I found a dark corner of the theater and pretended I had eyes to close.

2

Ashanda awoke. She took her time in between waking up and sitting up, and turned the radio back on last. No good morning this morning. She asks me what time it is and when she doesn't like the answer she goes back to sleep for another hour.

She leaves the theater by the back door, walks to the car, and drives to a McDonalds, where she goes directly to the restroom carrying her duffle bag and comes out a while later in different clothes. She buys coffee and drinks it sitting in the middle of a big orange plastic corner booth. There's a family of good American churchgoers sitting at one of the tables on the other side of the restaurant, Dad's wearing a polo shirt and gelled hair parted to the right and mom's wearing the only pair of yoga pants I've seen this far from a major urban area. Mom and Dad join the teenager at the cash register and the retiree in the T-shirt with the rainbow in staring at Ashanda as if she's an alien from another planet upon whom the Earth has declared war. She responds by not responding. She's somewhere else, somewhere serious, somewhere not here.

Once the caffeine is in her system, she leaves and drives to the historical society, still deep in thought. Every so often, she says something under her breath I can't hear or figure out. She asks me directions, only the second thing she's said to me since she woke up this morning, and once she knows exactly where the historical society is, she parks a couple of blocks away.

The historical society is a house among other houses; if it weren't for a modest wooden sign in the front yard, you'd walk right past it. A woman in a blue sun dress is unlocking the door.

Her hair is done up in a bun and she's wearing glasses with big light blue plastic frames. She's pushing the schoolmarm thing to the point of parody; she's either older or younger than she looks and I wouldn't put money down either way.

"Excuse me, m'am?" Ashanda's almost skipping by the time she reaches the society. Her voice is just a little nervous and a little scared, and a little excited and not quite all the way towards admitting that anything might go wrong. It's as calculated as a computer virus. I realize that she's been planning her pitch all morning.

"My name is Ashanda." The lady in the blue dress is trying to keep some professional distance, but Ashanda is a lost puppy and she's already caving before Ashanda has even said what she wants. "I was really hoping you could help me with something."

The lady in blue with the glasses- her name is Michelle- has pretty much lost the game by the time the two of them get through the door of the historical society. By the time they're inside she's already sitting Ashanda down and serving her tea and wanting to know how her trip has been so far, sweetheart. The gushing stops for a moment when Ashanda puts the rubbing of Ethan Pale's tombstone on the table.

"Very interesting man. We have a file on him. Do you mind if I ask what your interest is, Ashanda?"

Ashanda looks meaningfully into her cup before she brings her big brown eyes back into position.

"I think he might have been my grandfather."

Michelle sits up straight. It's like she's got a string glued to the top of her head and somebody yanked on it.

"Well. That is provocative."

Ashanda doesn't crack for a second. Give the girl an Oscar.

Michelle comes back with a folder full of old pictures and press clippings. Ethan Pale looked a little like an Okie, he looked a little Italian, he had shoulders like somebody who worked for a living but hands that seemed to be the product of expensive piano lessons. In black and white, he looked like a matinee idol with dirt on his face. Ethan Pale the radical man of the people, leading the union singalong around the fire.

"He didn't record much, but he was very influential. And if you ask around every so often you run into somebody who still knows his songs, even if they don't know anything about him."

Ashanda lets her go on for a long time before interrupting. "He's buried less than a mile away. Did he have family around here?"

"He spent his last years in the area. It's not clear if it was a case of him coming back to his childhood home or if it was something else; there's not a lot to go on. The paper trail dies when he stopped performing and doesn't pick up again until his obituary."

"Do we know who paid for his cemetery plot?"

"We do not. It's very frustrating. Someone got rid of the records. Just threw them in the trash."

"You know an awful lot about him."

Michelle doesn't blush exactly, but she does smile like that.

"I guess I do. You'll have to excuse me if I sounded a little defensive at first, I'm a little protective of Ethan. It must sound silly, there's only three records you can listen to anymore. But that was enough for me." She pulled out one of the pictures. Ethan's in the foreground, playing guitar, tilting his head up like the sky were his microphone. There's a circle of people sitting around him, but the only one in you can see in the picture is a girl with black hair. She's twisting her pony tail with both hands and looking up at him like he's Marlon Brando or Santa or God.

"When I was just a kid checking things out from the library, I envied that girl. I don't know how you can listen to 'Prairie Rose' and not want to get a little closer to the man singing it."

Michelle smiles at Ashanda, looking for something in return that Ashanda is a second late in providing, the first false step I've seen her make today. Ashanda tries to recover.

"He was something. I just wish I knew more about him."

Michelle goes with it. She's invested; she wants to keep the wheels turning. "Well that's totally understandable. There's a story there, of course you want to know what it is. It's family." She leans back in her chair and stares into space. Important decision-making position. She doesn't spend too long there. "How long do you have for your investigation, Ashanda?"

"Time's not an issue. But I've only got enough gas in the tank to head home and I'm kind of broke." Michelle shifts just a little and Ashanda steps on it right away. "I don't accept charity." Michelle relaxes. Nobody wants to be made a sucker of.

"I understand. I was just thinking of putting you in touch with someone I know over in Decatur. She volunteers for the historical society there, we met at a convention. One of the sisterhood, you know. She has some Ethan Pale documents too, it was how we first met. But it might have to wait if you don't have a way to get there right now."

Ashanda doesn't fight it. I really hope she's not giving up that easy, but she's a closed book. If there's a strategy I don't see it.

"That kind of sucks. I won't have as much free time once I start working again."

"What do you do, Ashanda? If you don't mind me asking. I would think that you're a student, but school would be in session right now."

"I'm a psychic," Ashanda says. The book opens a crack. There's no way to finesse this; either Michelle buys it or she doesn't.

Michelle's eyebrows pop up and she takes a long sip of tea.

"You tell the future? Professionally?"

Ashanda is modest. She explains, respectfully, like Michelle were a college admissions counselor. "I don't have that particular gift. Sometimes I can steer a person in the right direction with tarot or with some kind of an intermediary, but what I do most often is connect my clients to the spirits of the departed. That's what I'm good at."

For a moment, I want to armchair quarterback- why not tell her you can predict the future, you're going to be blowing town in a few hours anyway- but I get over the impulse quickly. Michelle thinks it over.

"You're an interesting young woman, Ashanda." Michelle smiles at her. Ashanda smiles back sheepishly, shrugs her shoulders, bringing back just a little bit of the lost puppy. It's a killing blow. They spend the rest of the morning talking.

The plan is in place by the time they leave the historical society. They go to Michelle's house for lunch and Ashanda changes into her earth-mama work clothes. Then they go to the mall.

The mall in Mattoon is a strange beast. It is a mall; it's got all the usual mall stuff, with only a few more empty storefronts than you might expect. But it also has a flea market crammed into it, folding tables in all the walkways and extra corners. There are no signs that this is a special occasion, they've just got chocolate in their peanut butter permanently. A man in fatigues is manning a station right by the door Michelle and Ashanda come in at. He's selling books, mostly related to gun control, and military uniforms, and he has a smaller adjacent table loaded to capacity with old roleplaying games and crates full of dice. Michelle pointedly switches place with Ashanda as they make the left turn past him into the mall, so that she is in between Ashanda and army-man's dagger-eyes. He tracks the both of them as they walk away. No terrorism on his watch, I guess.

I take the floating tour. There's another table in another wing of the mall, manned by a malnourished teenage boy in a sweatshirt, which sells weapons, your normal selection of machetes and katanas and brass knuckles along with a few items from a brand called Zombie Killer, which makes serrated knives and punching daggers with neon green plastic handles and an inlaid biohazard logo. He stares at Ashanda too, but he mostly just perseverates on her ass and tries to process his feelings. Nothing else stands out as a potential threat. Books, DVDs, homemade pottery, paintings of cats. There's one table full of handmade wooden crosses, carved meticulously with patterns and Celtic knots.

Michelle heads over to the security office, tucked in an odd corner next to the restrooms and a barber shop. I eavesdrop while Ashanda stays back at a polite distance. Michelle has a table where she sells used books and perfume on Saturday afternoons. Nobody's using it now.

Ashanda lays out her tarot cards. A quick trip to the drug store for posterboard and markers and they have a sign. It's slow at first. A few people trickle over. Ashanda does her thing. She gets a few more, a few more, a few more. A line forms. By the time the mall closes, she's got three-hundred dollars in her pocket.

3

Ashanda sleeps over at Michelle's place. Any remaining awkwardness is gone by the time they leave the mall and the two of them are like middle schoolers at a sleepover for the rest of the night. Ashanda has never seen Casablanca. Michelle cracks open a bottle of wine without thinking it through. She asks Ashanda if she's ever had a drink before and Ashanda tells her it's been a few years. That's enough for Michelle. She makes a comment later about what an exciting birthday twenty must have been and Ashanda doesn't say a word.

The movie ends and the bottle's most of the way towards being empty.

Michelle: "You've been polite enough not to mention Luke."

Even inebriated, Ashanda's poker face doesn't slip.

"He's been polite tonight," Michelle says.

Ashanda understands. "Not making too much noise?"

"Not too much. He was always good about that. When it was girls' night, he knew to make himself scarce."

"Good for him."

"Good for him indeed. I remember the funeral, all these people telling me that he was in a better place now, licking their lips to see if they could finally get me coming to church. He's not in a better place; he's with me. What's he going to do in Heaven, play the harp?" Michelle finishes her glass. "Pardon me. Oversharing."

"It's all right." I have no idea what Ashanda is thinking.

"You're being kind to me. What a day, huh?"

Michelle talks a little more about her husband. Just to satisfy my own curiosity, I take a quick tour of the house, attic to foundations. There's nothing there but wood and drywall and old pictures.

4

Michelle has a couch that folds out; Ashanda sleeps there. The morning arrives, and is inevitably a little more awkward than the night before, but they leave as friends. Hugs, breakfast, Michelle watching from her porch as Ashanda drives around the corner.

Ashanda worms her way towards the highway. Left turn, right turn, left turn, right turn. She turns on the radio. She gets static, but doesn't adjust the dial.

"How am I ever going to talk to her again?"

Talking through the speakers feels like stretching my legs after a cramped flight.

"What do you mean?"

"I was working her. I was running a game and she treated me like we're friends."

"Aren't you friends?"

"I have no idea."

"Do you want to be?"

"Every time from now on that I see her or hear her voice or look at something in her handwriting, I'm going to have to think about what a manipulative bitch I am."

"I think maybe you're taking this a little far."

"Well fuck you then." Ashanda reaches for the dial. She stops, thinks, and brings her hand back without turning off the radio.

"Okay, excuse me, I apologize for that, but do you see how this might be a little more complicated than you're making it sound?"

"What did you do? You asked for help. Maybe you hammed it up a little when you first went up to her, but so what? She's not stupid."

"Tell me that her husband was in that house. Go ahead, tell me."

"Sounds like you don't think he was."

"I don't think I'm wrong, either."

"You're not."

"So I'm lying to her. I'm lying to her so I can sleep on her couch."

"I don't think she would have kicked you out if you'd told her her that husband wasn't really a ghost."

"How the hell do you know that?"

"Because she liked you a lot. She thought you were something and she thought it was something that you were staying with her. You can argue with me if you want, but you wouldn't have brought it up if you didn't want a second opinion and it seemed pretty obvious to me."

She leaves the radio on but says nothing. Awkward silence. And it's not going anywhere, so I keep talking. I'm surprised by what comes out.

"When I was your age, I thought everybody liked me. My father was a powerful man. At least by his own standards, I know now that there's always somebody who's a bigger deal than you, but he was the biggest fish in his own pond. I was his only son. He always kept me around. When I was little I didn't think about that, it was just how things were, but later I got the idea in my head that maybe it was me, maybe I was special. And maybe that's why everybody was being so nice.

"It was decades later before I figured out what was really going on. My father loved me. He really did. But I wasn't the kind of person he would respect in the absence of that love. He kept me around to show off. It was like leaving the door to his house unlocked. It was a dare. You want to fuck with my wimpy record collector of a son? Go ahead, see what happens. So every pat on the back, every 'Hey Charlie how ya doin?' , that's what was really going on."

I stop and it's awkward again, and this time I leave it to her. She picks it up quickly.

"Is there a point to you telling me all this, Charlie?"

"I guess not. Just that if you really want to know what I think, consider the source. And I don't think you have anything to feel guilty about."

We're on the highway now, on an empty patch, nothing but endless rows of corn on either side of us. Early morning traffic.

"I don't know what it is about dead people," Ashanda says. "Whenever they're not bitching, they're giving advice."

"You say dead people when you mean old people."

"Same difference."

"So this is my reward for trying to make you feel better about yourself?"

"I turned a deck of cards into three hundred dollars yesterday and I got to keep the cards. I feel great about myself."

"Glad to hear. I'm relieved, honestly."

There's nothing on the radio but country music and people arguing about politics. Ashanda makes a request, and I see to it that the rest of the drive out of Mattoon becomes an Al Green marathon.

5

Ashanda stops for lunch at a straight-up no-bullshit waitresses-in-aprons eggs-and-bacon diner just outside city limits. Patsy is playing on the digital jukebox in the corner. I'm happy to report that her server is incredibly sweet and asks Ashanda how her trip is going and calls her hun.

Ashanda orders the corned beef hash skillet and heads to the bathroom once the waitress leaves with her order. A few minutes after she leaves her seat, a caravan pulls into the parking lot that the diner shares with the gas station next door. Two black Jeeps followed by a limo followed by another Jeep. They all have tinted windows and look like they just got waxed.

They stop- they don't park, they just stop, a long diagonal line ignoring the paint. A man in overalls climbs down from the passenger side of the lead jeep. There are murmurings from the diner as people notice the new arrivals. Somebody wonders if they're rock stars.

The doors to the first two jeeps all open at the same time. Five guys in overalls climb out of each one. They're all dead. One of them is missing an arm and has the sleeve of his work shirt tied into a knot. The knot is stained almost black, with patches of red and yellow.

Five of them head towards the gas station, and the other five heads towards us. There are two front entrances to the restaurant. Two guys take each of them while the fifth heads around to the back. The guys by the front doors stand shoulder to shoulder, blocking the way. There's more whispers, looks around for the hidden cameras, jokes about horror movies. That's really good zombie makeup, a kid says. A waitress heads over to see what the hell is going on.

Gary gets out of the limo. He's wearing a gold lame suit with a silver tie, ready for Vegas. He is embodied- he opens the door, closes the door, his feet touch down on the parking lot in his sparkly shoes. He walks over to where Ashanda parked our car and takes a look at the license plate. I'm too far away to see him smile, but still I can picture the exact look on his face.

Ashanda's still in the bathroom. When I go in she's washing her hands. I yell but she can't hear me. She forgot to turn on her Walkman. Patsy's song comes to an end. He's walking by, she's falling to pieces.

CHAPTER 10

1

Ashanda washed up. The sink was so close to the door that she almost hit her elbow into the wall each time she put one hand on top of the other.

The music stopped and started again. Ashanda heard bongos and smiled. Charlie was having some fun. She pressed the dryer button and heard the singer start in over the hot air blowing. A boy wanted a girl, but the music wasn't happy, something bad was going to happen. She heard one line:

"Of loving..." He held it long enough that it became its own sentence. "...a stranger, even though it can endanger..."

Danger.

"Charlie?"

No answer. She checked her Walkman and turned it back on.

"Gary's here. He's got the building surrounded."

"How's the car?"

"They're right on top of it."

The restroom was in the far back corner of the restaurant, next to the rear kitchen entrance. "Can I open the door?"

"Yeah. They're not inside. They're just keeping anybody else from leaving."

She cracked the door open, then pushed it. She could hear something over the music. Two things. A voice on a megaphone, and somebody getting the shit kicked out of them. Grabbing, shoving, grunting, yelling interrupted by hitting.

She dropped down to her hands and knees and crawled towards the front of the restaurant. When she reached the end of the hallway, the back of a booth still gave her some cover. She took a very quick look around the booth, just enough to see a split second of three large men in overalls looking down towards the floor.

"That's the thing about fucking football players."

His voice echoed through the megaphone. She couldn't see him, had never heard the voice before, but she knew who he was.

"You catch one of those guys alone, like you're stuck in an elevator or something, and they're nice and friendly and make you think you got the wrong idea, but the second there's anybody else in the room they're laughing at you and snapping towels at your balls before gym class."

Ashanda immediately gave up on figuring out what the fuck he was talking about, but kept listening.

"Anyway. I'd tell you to send out your special buddy, but I'm once again forced to admit that I don't actually want you to do that, because if you grow a brain cell and give her up it means I don't get to do what I'm gonna do if you don't grow a brain cell and give her up. Because I have to say, this is going to be awesome. I don't know why the brunette never did shit like this, I guess she just didn't know how to have fun. Maddie, go ahead and do your thing. Start with the gas station."

She heard the people in the restaurant whispering and then yelling. Something about gas. Orange gas.

Ashanda crawled backwards to the hallway and stood up. She heard someone begging her boyfriend or husband or whoever not to get up. She looked back at the bathroom, then the closed janitor's closet, and then the open door to the kitchen.

She heard the people yelling, giving up on any hope that keeping quiet would make it go away, and Gary laughing through the megaphone. The world got slippery, the way it did when everything was going wrong at once and Ashanda knew she might die. Like falling asleep. You never remember the moment you stop being awake. It's a surprise every time it happens.

Ashanda remembered getting locked in a closet while a man beat on her mother. She remembered feeling like she would suffocate, wondering if the closet was air tight the way you did when you were little and could casually doubt the laws of physics.

Four in front, one in the back, through the kitchen. She'd go through the kitchen. If they can touch me, I can touch them.

She ducked down and poked her head into the kitchen.

Charlie: "It's empty, the staff headed up towards the register. The guy is still by the back door. He's looking in; if you go across he'll see you."

She looked across the room to the counter by the sink. There was a long magnetic strip on the wall. A row of knives led neatly to a meat cleaver with a blade the size of her face.

She took a moment to get in character, and when she stumbled into the kitchen she was shell-shocked, she didn't know what was going on, she was too confused to cry. She heard heavy work-boot footsteps coming up behind her and didn't turn towards them.

Something grabbed her shoulder. She dropped the act, grabbed the meat cleaver off the wall, and turned. Her shirt ripped. She cut down and didn't quite cut off its hand; the smell stabbed up into her nose, like opening a Tupperware container after six months in back of the fridge. She stepped back and swung down with both hands, chopping firewood. The cleaver lodged itself in the thing's skull. Ashanda ran past it. The door was open.

A sad excuse for a swamp started where the parking lot ended, reeds sticking up from mud. She kept running. She heard heavy footsteps behind her, faster than she'd hoped. It tackled her from behind and she turned her face to the side as she went down so she wouldn't break any teeth.

She tried to get loose and only managed to turn around, so that her back was pinned against the ground and her arms were trapped under its legs. Its face looked like it had been left on a grill, and the cleaver was sticking straight up from its forehead like a tiara. It put its hands on Ashanda's throat. Only the right one still worked but that was enough. She couldn't breathe.

The world changed again, as she started to leave it. Everything was fine. She would've laughed. She should've just died in the closet when she was ten, it would have been the same thing. Her whole life, everything that had happened; there were words for it, something she'd heard at school. She couldn't remember the words.

Lightning crashed and the dead man's head exploded, covering her with bile. She gasped and got up and had a headache.

Across the parking lot was a giant man in a state trooper's uniform. He had a tidy bullet hole in his forehead and three more in his chest. His uniform was fresh pressed and clean from the knees up, and dirty and ragged below that. His boots had fallen to pieces, and his feet were covered with scabs and calluses, layers of them. Like he'd been walking on hot coals for years.

"I can tell you how Gary did it," the cop said. "Meet me in four days at the crossroads. Charlie knows where."

Ashanda didn't move.

"I'll tell them I tried to shoot you and hit him by accident. I'll tell them you went that way." He pointed. "Go that way instead." He pointed again. "Go now."

Ashanda heard more heavy footsteps coming. Then she did what the man said.

She didn't know how long it took. Her shirt got caught on a branch and ripped again, and she could feel mud splashing all over her with every step. She ran across a two-lane road with no signs, into the woods on the other side. She ran until she couldn't run any more. She tried to ask a question but she was breathing too hard. Charlie figured it out.

"I think you're clear," he said. "They're still looking for you in the swamp."

She tried to sit down by a tree and ended up laying down instead.

All the circles and the running around, and it ends with her getting strangled in a gas station parking lot. She remembered it, that thing she'd heard at school. It was something Mr. Anatol had said. A shaggy dog story. Her whole life.

2

Charlie sounded guilty when he told her that they'd better get moving. All of her stuff had been in the car, but she still had the rest of her money in her pocket. There was a Walmart a mile away. Charlie led her to it. She walked in through the sliding doors. Her shirt had two gaping holes, her face and chest were covered with something that split the difference between blood and compost, and she was splattered with mud from the waist down. The greeter got halfway through her greeting and then just stared as Ashanda walked the rest of the way in.

She bought clothes, batteries, shoes, toiletries, and a backpack. She was followed by a manager the entire time she was in the store. He hovered about twenty yards away and pretended to be doing something else. Whenever she turned a corner, she heard him scramble into a position where he could see her again. She paid for everything, went into the public bathroom, locked the door, cleaned herself off as best she could, changed clothes, and left her old stuff in the garbage can.

There was a Chinese buffet on the other side of the same development as the Walmart. Ashanda paid for a meal and stayed there for two hours, until her hands weren't shaking any more. She demolished three plates quickly and spent her last forty-five minutes nursing a bowl of chocolate pudding. She saw the lady at the cash register glance over at her a few times.

A guy in an apron came out from the kitchen. He was obese to the point that his apron barely wrapped around him and had visible trouble walking. He came over to her table. She waited for it, tried to decide if she'd even fight it or just let him kick her out.

"Are you doing all right, sweetheart?"

"I'm fine," she said softly. She wanted to go to sleep. She didn't want this asshole to kick her out of the restaurant.

"Glad to hear. Take all the time you need."

It took her a moment to process what he'd just said.

"And if you need a ride someplace. Hospital, cops, whatever. There's a shelter not too far from here. Not prying, but if you do need a lift, it's not a problem."

She had just enough time to look him in the eye and realize he wasn't kidding. At that point, he was already turning back towards the kitchen, slowly like a ship in a port.

Ashanda touched her neck and figured it out. The bruises were just getting colorful. Part of her was grateful, and part of her couldn't help but be pissed off that she looked like somebody who needed a ride to a shelter. Cookies at Christmas again.

She finished her pudding and slid her headphones over her ears.

"Gary."

"Yup. That was our guy."

"Any idea why he was talking about football players?"

"Nope. I'm coming up blank on the suit, too."

"He was wearing a suit?"

"Yeah, you missed that part. Trust me, it's a good thing. It would have made things more traumatic."

"You know the dead cop?"

"We used to work together but I don't actually know him all that well. He might not be my biggest fan. I kind of screwed him over."

"You know where the crossroads is?"

"I do. We can head to Decatur, follow up on Mr. Pale, and still make it up there with time to spare."

Ashanda pulled out her phone and stared at it. The power was off.

"I thought you and Betty weren't going to call each other."

"That had been the plan."

Ashanda stared at the phone a little while longer. She turned it on, but she didn't dial a number. She went on the Internet instead.

"That's funny," she said.

"I can't see the screen, what's funny?"

"Ethan Pale. He's been dead for about fifty years, right?"

"He never made my playlist, but that's what the archivist said."

"He has a show in Peoria in three days."

3

Ashanda called Betty. They kept it short. Betty wanted to know if things had gotten serious on her end. Ashanda told her that they had. Ashanda wanted to know how Betty was doing. Betty was spare on details. The box had been enough to keep her safe for a while, and then she'd gotten word from a client that something worse was coming and that she'd better get out of town. She was in a safe place now, somewhere nobody would think to look. It was better for both of them if they each didn't know where the other was.

Betty said "I love you" and Ashanda said the same. Ashanda hung up the phone. Her headache was back. She didn't think she could fit another ounce of food into her body. She rested her head on the table and took a twenty minute nap.

She woke up, checked how much time had gone by, and approached the door that led to the kitchen. The cook had a lunch break in half an hour. She grabbed a few more cookies and waited.

It was an Embassy Suites, which would have been way over the line for what she'd be willing to pay for usually, but it was where she was. The cook's name was David and he asked her if she was underage before she had a chance to think about how she was going to get a room. He checked out the room, put it on his credit card, and took cash from her to make up the difference. He almost raised an eyebrow when he saw how much money she had, but didn't say anything about it. He didn't say much of anything. Whatever reason he had for helping her out, he didn't say. He wished her good luck, reminded her one more time about that shelter, and drove back to work.

The hotel had a swimming pool. She didn't have a suit, but she was tempted to figure something out. She took a long hot shower instead.

She watched the local news. They were refreshingly candid about admitting that they had no idea what the hell had gone on at the diner. The place had been stormed by men in masks who held the place up, beat the shit out of the only guy who didn't do what they said, used some kind of poison gas on the people in the gas station nearby, and then left. They didn't take any money. There was an APB out for black Jeeps, but no luck so far.

She went to sleep, and got up very early the next morning. There was a little stand by the front door with fliers for a cab company. There was also a shuttle that went from the train station to the Decatur airport. She called, she waited, the cab arrived. From there another shuttle took her where she wanted to go. The trip took about two and a half times as long as it would have if she'd just driven, but she used the time to make a phone call.

4

You could build a pretty good model of downtown Mattoon using only cardboard boxes. The buildings were all three stories tall and didn't need to be; most of them were occupied, but above the first floor were nothing but black windows. Walking around, Ashanda kept getting the feeling that if she looked at the right angle she'd see that they were all props with nothing behind them but scaffolding. She kept expecting to turn a corner and see guys in cowboy hats facing off.

There was a fountain in the middle of town with a little brick building next to it that advertised itself as the town visitors' center. There was just enough room inside for a pair of public bathrooms, a drinking fountain, a wall full of books and fliers and a desk with a short woman with long red hair and glasses sitting behind it. Everything was clean and tidy, each stack of books was perfectly flush.

The woman at the desk looked up just as Ashanda started thinking about how to get her attention.

"You're Ashanda," she said, sounding like a witness in court. "Michelle's friend. We spoke over the phone."

That'd been exactly what Ashanda was going to say, and now she didn't know how to answer. "Yeah, that's me."

"Excellent. Come this way. I'm Terese."

Terese turned the sign on the door from open to closed, held it open until Ashanda got the idea to step back outside, and locked the door. She walked past the fountain. Tunnel vision, straight ahead. Ashanda followed her.

They came to an unmarked wooden door down the street from a place that sold paintings and jewelry. Terese unlocked it and they went through to a wooden stairwell with yellow walls, going up. There was a thin layer of dust on each step, and when Ashanda looked closely for a second she could see another, older set of footprints, still sitting there in the dust.

The stairwell led to a single door. Stepping through it transported the two of them seventy years back in time. A few pieces of furniture were broken, things were dusty, things needed to be polished. But red velvet was red velvet, and the crystal chandelier hanging from the ceiling was almost big enough to live in. There were two full bars that still had bottles behind them, mirrors on every wall and parts of the ceiling. A hundred little hidden corners.

"They're all like this, all the buildings. Street level was main street, and that's as far as the cops went. Everything above that was speakeasies and brothels."

Ashanda's mind ran a few laps. There was no question she could ask that wouldn't sound stupid, so she just asked them.

"Why is all of this still here?"

"Who's going to get rid of it? If the town council had any imagination they'd open a museum, and if a developer ever thought it was worth the trouble, then the bulldozers would take care of it. But neither of those is going to happen any time soon. This is a just a tiny all-American town. We can't keep two movie theaters open at the same time without booze and hookers."

Ashanda didn't think of herself as somebody who blushed, but she saw Terese's eyes sparkle and she knew she'd lost the game for a moment.

Terese let it ride. She was getting a kick out of this. "You wanted to know about Ethan Pale. You're going to want to see this. This is one of the good parts."

Around the corner was a bulletin board covered with paper, old paper, all the pins metal and none of them plastic. Newspaper clippings, black and white pictures. Some of the corners had curled and gone yellow. Others seemed frozen in time, like somebody had put them up just the other day.

Ashanda had to look twice to see his face. There he was, and there he was again, and there he was shaking a man's hand who looked so much like a bad guy on The Untouchables it was like he was trolling law enforcement. This was a different Ethan Pale. He was wearing a different suit in each picture, sometimes matching the band he was in and sometimes a little flashier. The grease in his hair shined through newsprint and across decades.

"He played in the big bands before he was ever a folk singer. You couldn't really be a star that way, though. He switched up later and if the first part of his career ended up on a record we don't know about it." Terese took a few steps closer so that she was standing next to Ashanda, looking at the board together. "Michelle doesn't like it. She likes the legend, that he was raised on a farm and learned to play guitar from some old blues man." She said 'blues man' like it was something profoundly silly. A unicycle racer, or a boxing kangaroo.

Ashanda reached for her pocket where her phone was, then hesitated and looked back over at Terese.

"No flash," Terese said, serious again. Ashanda took pictures.

And that was it. Once Terese had had her opportunity to show off, she wasn't interested in much else. Ashanda thanked her and she said it wasn't a big deal, and that she had to get back to work.

The bus station was a short walk from downtown, and they had a line that went straight to Peoria. The station was crowded and she had to wait for a couple of hours, but once she was on the bus, she had enough privacy to talk to Charlie without anyone looking at her twice.

"We've got time to get to the show and make our other appointment?"

"It shouldn't be a problem."

"Have you ever heard of this guy? Good or bad, have you heard his music?"

"Nope. Before my time."

Ashanda looked out at the rolling fields and tried unsuccessfully to find something she'd never seen before.

"I'm going to try to get some sleep, Charlie. Wake me up if zombies attack the bus."

"Sure thing. You want any good night music?"

She'd already passed out.

CHAPTER 11

I'll spare you the endless descriptions of cows and windmills. We made it to Peoria. Nobody got hurt, no weird shit happened. We had plenty of time to spare, which was good because it was a long walk from the bus station to the campus coffee shop where Mr. Pale was scheduled to appear that evening. Ashanda still got there early. She walked around campus and fit in like a glove. If I'd had the power to do so, I'd have been tempted to elbow passing sophomores in the ribs and telling them the girl drinking hot chocolate in the corner tried to chop off somebody's hand with a meat cleaver two days ago. Just to watch the looks on their faces, just to see them not believe it.

The coffee shop is in the basement of the building that has the financial aide office and all the student mailboxes. Ashanda grabs one of the comfortable chairs , enjoys her drink and listens to the campus music station playing from the speakers in the ceiling. The DJ offers to play requests and Ashanda calls in and asks for "Prairie Rose".

She listens, I listen and watch her listen.

The song ends. Ashanda slides her headphones down over her ears.

"I don't get it."

I know what she means. It was a folk song. It was about a girl.

"It wasn't bad. I don't know if it's a hit, but it's a nice little song."

"The girls in the picture looked like they were about to jump him."

"I don't know what to tell you. These things are subjective. David Cassidy used to drive the ladies out of their minds."

She looks up a picture of David Cassidy on her phone and thinks it's pretty funny. We shoot the shit about it for an hour or so.

People start trickling in for the concert. The cashier sets up a microphone and a chair in a corner of the room. Ashanda already has a perfect seat. All she has to do is keep it.

One last thing. I'm going to be straightforward about this, so there's no confusion. Once the room is full- and it is full by the time the concert starts, standing room only- Ethan Pale comes out from the tiny excuse for a green room they have behind the counter. It's him, the guy from the picture. You could convince yourself that he was a really good impersonator, if that's what you had to believe. But that's not what it is. It's him. It's the same guy.

And he's not a ghost. He's wearing a flannel shirt and conditions his hair, and the moment he opens his mouth to sing the whole room sinks into whatever's nearby like dogs in the summer. He's alive. His heart beats. And he hasn't aged a day.

That's all from me for a little bit. Enjoy the show.

CHAPTER 12

1

Ethan played "Prairie Rose" first. He wasn't even feeling it yet. He was still working- even though he was never working, he reminded himself. He never had to try. It just felt like it sometimes.

"Prairie Rose" ended and he started his next song without stopping. The first one hundred and twenty seconds were an instrumental. The crowd at the coffee shop was just big enough to make him feel good. Girls in front row. A dude with a mustache giving him the stink-eye from the back, another one with a ponytail doing the same thing from the other corner. Like it was a mistake that he was the one playing and they weren't.

I'm not even singing. You heard the song you came for, right? So go ahead and leave. I dare you.

Nobody left. He was winning. He smiled and some of them smiled back. Everybody loved everybody. Which was part of the way true, because they sure as hell loved him. And he was actually starting to warm to them, now, too. The girls were pretty. His punches were landing.

He reminded himself that he was young. He was playing a coffee shop, but that's what you did when you were young. Everything was just fine. He started singing.

Two sets with an intermission in between. Most of his best songs came in the first set, after his three starters and before the Weavers cover he threw in before the break to remind everyone what a good Ethan Pale impersonator he was. The second set was to make sure he got invited back, so that was when he'd start with the patter. For right now, he could do what he wanted. The crowd was in his pocket anyway.

He saw a black girl sitting in a comfy green chair next to the window. She was by herself and she was staring at him. It wasn't a look he could categorize. He didn't know what it meant.

Bolt from the blue. She knows.

Even when it came to him, he didn't miss a note.

He zombie-marched through the Weavers song and told everybody he'd be back in a few minutes. That wasn't quite right; he didn't really have any place to go, he just stepped down from the platform and over to the counter. He nodded his head politely at the applause. He drank ice water. A few of the girls told him how great he was and he smiled bashfully and thanked them.

The girl from the green chair was waiting behind the first row of admirers. They made eye contact and understood each other.

Ashanda waited for a quiet moment to step forward.

"We need to talk."

Ethan smiled.

"I'm glad you're enjoying the show."

He got back behind the microphone. People found their seats and settled down. Ashanda sat back down in the green chair and whispered something no one could hear to someone no one could see. Ethan leaned in.

"Thank you so much, you're wonderful. This next song I'm going to play..."

Feedback. Ashanda was the only member of the audience that didn't flinch.

Ethan cleared his throat. "Sorry about that, folks. As I was saying..."

It happened four more times. Once in the middle of a song. Ashanda approached Ethan again after the set was over and the crowd was starting to leave.

"This could be every show you do from now on. We need to talk."

2

Ethan and Ashanda found a twenty-four hour Mexican restaurant just off campus. They took a booth- they had their choice, they were the only customers. The waitress switched off between taking care of them, mopping the floor, and checking on her son and his video game behind the counter.

"What do you want to know exactly? I don't want to waste your time."

"You can start by telling me how you came back from the dead."

"Gary did it."

"Okay. How?"

"I have no idea."

"How about why?"

"I'm not entirely sure."

"Then you're partially sure. Tell me what you think."

Their food arrived. Ethan gathered his courage and adjusted his hair.

"When I was..."

"Dead," Ashanda said. Ethan shrugged.

"All I did was play. I couldn't stop. No matter how tired I was, I had to keep on going. There was an audience, but when I wanted to see their faces everything was a blur, and when I wanted to hide everything got sharper and it felt like their eyes were cutting through me.

"I don't know how long it was like that, but it was a long time.

"Then something changed. I could see a face in the crowd, this beautiful woman with brown hair. Someone could hear me again. So I played for her. She wasn't there all the time, but even when she wasn't, things got better. I could stop and rest sometimes. And it wasn't as cold.

"She came up and talked to me during my breaks, and that was when I figured out that she was in charge. I started sucking up to her a little bit. I played what she wanted to hear. I wrote her songs. And she made things better for me, more comfortable."

He tried to figure out how much he would tell and how much he would leave out. He didn't try to conceal what he was doing.

"After a while, she started asking me what I wanted. She wanted to give me what I wanted. You know how that goes, right? I don't even know you, but I can tell. The thing was, the only thing I really wanted was to not be dead any more. I didn't think it was possible, but one time I made a joke and I saw the look in her eyes. So from then on that was the plan. I didn't smile as much. I played but I didn't play quite like I used to. I told a story. I got a little worse, and a little worse, and a little worse.

"And it worked. She got worried. She started giving me presents. We went to the beach, some European painter's version of a tropical island. We drank wine and ate caviar. She made the crowds I was playing to look bigger. She was like a rich dad who never spends time with his kids and feels guilty, I think she would've given me a pony if I'd asked for one. But whatever she did, it was still cold; I could tell it wasn't real. I knew she was holding out on me.

"Finally I put my cards on the table. I told her she could try and distract me all she wanted, but I only wanted one thing, and I knew she could give it to me if she tried. And if she didn't give me that one thing, there was nothing I could do about it, she had all the cards and she could make me dance like a monkey if she wanted to, but if she really loved me..."

That was a mistake, he hadn't meant to let that go. He looked to Ashanda for something, anything, punishment would have been fine, but her face was an ice sculpture. He picked it up again once he saw she wasn't going to yell at him.

"She went away for a while, and when she came back, she told me it wasn't going to happen. She almost cried. She said she couldn't give me that, but she could give me everything else. This is where things get fuzzy, I don't remember this part so well. It wasn't like before, where she was putting on a show for me. I was calling the shots, not all of them, but some of them. She said she wanted the two of us to be equals, she didn't want the wall in between us anymore.

"I'd still play 'Prairie Rose' for her sometimes. Just to show her I cared.

Ethan and Ashanda were done eating. The waitress dropped off the check and went back over to check on her son.

"You've been talking for a long time and you still haven't answered my question," Ashanda said.

"Patience, sweetheart. A man with no skin came to visit me. I can tell by how you're looking at me right now that you know him, but I didn't. We were in a room with a table. He had a contract and a red pen. He told me he could bring me back to life. Quid quo pro. I give him what the brunette gave me, and he'd do what she couldn't."

"And you signed."

"I did. When I opened my eyes I was in a homeless shelter in San Berdino. I had the clothes on my back and an acoustic. Nothing weird since then, I've just been doing my thing."

Ashanda got out her phone and flipped through to the pictures of Ethan in a suit. She slid the phone to the other side of the table.

"These are all you?"

Ethan picked up the phone and moved through the pictures. It took him a while but he knew what he was doing.

He finished off his Coke and slid the glass to the side of the table for a refill. He'd been doing that all night.

"Wow. These do take me back."

"How'd you make the switch to being a folk singer?"

"You know how boxers change weight classes? When they've stepped on everybody at middleweight, so they put on twenty pounds so they can step on everybody at heavyweight too?" He gave her back the phone. "I'm a guitar player. A style is just a style." He slid out from the booth. "Men's room. I'll be right back."

"Fine," Ashanda said, but he was already gone.

Ashanda reached into her pocket for her headphones.

"Charlie?"

"Yup."

"You're sure he's not a ghost."

"Nope. He's a flesh and blood human being."

Ethan's jacket was piled on the inside of his seat. Ashanda pulled it across the table. His car keys were in his inside lapel pocket. She took them and left the restaurant.

There was a guitar case and a duffel bag in the back seat. Ashanda left them on the ground next to where the car had been parked when she drove away.

It wasn't far to the highway. Ashanda imagined Ethan filing a police report with a dead guy's face and a decades-old Social Security number. It was good to be cheered up, even just for a moment.

"How far are we from our appointment, Charlie?"

They weren't far. Plenty of time to grab a hotel room. They weren't due at the crossroads until tomorrow night.

3

At the hotel, Ashanda went to bed, slept for four hours, and woke up. She looked out at the parking lot through the curtains and talked to Charlie.

"There is something I want to tell you," Charlie said. "I lied to you before." He told her about the football player and what he'd done.

"Just because you were bored?"

"Looking back, yeah. That was the reason."

She wasn't mad and wasn't sure why. Maybe it was just because she was tired, maybe her brain wasn't working the way it was supposed to. "Why are you telling me this now?"

"Listening to Ethan got under my skin. Somehow we got pretty far along without lying to each other and I don't want to be the one to break the streak."

"Do you want to keep being honest?"

"I guess I do."

"Are we really going to make it through this? Even if we figure out what happened, are we going to be able to do anything about it?"

"It depends what my old co-worker has to tell us. If he's blowing hot air or if what he has to say doesn't help as much as he seems to think it will, then I don't know what we'll do next."

Ashanda closed the curtain and laid back down on the bed, over the covers. She closed her eyes. She imagined a knock on the door, looking out the window and seeing nothing but a crowd of overalls waiting for her. She knew staying awake wasn't going to help anything, but she could still feel the sore spots on her neck.

"I wasn't going to figure it out. You didn't have to tell me."

"If it weren't for me, you never would have been in danger in the first place."

"Well, no shit. But just the same." She opened her eyes back up and looked closely at the dark ceiling.

"Are you as scared as I am?"

"I doubt it," Charlie said.

That made Ashanda laugh. It shook something loose, and her eyes closed by themselves not long after.

CHAPTER 13

1

Nobody I met ever made up the rules for my old job. The one with the crystals hanging from the rear view mirror, you remember that, right? There was a path you followed, and if you followed it in the right way and at the right time I was allowed to pass messages along from one side to another. The path predated my awareness of it. It predated the highway and I'm pretty sure it was around before any of the people that were responsible for managing it. When the brunette gave me the job, I asked her why it had to be the way that it was. If people want to pass notes from one side to the other, why not just let them? Or don't let them. Most people don't get to talk to their dead aunt or whoever and they muddle along. Why did it have to be "sometimes, when the moon is right"? I didn't see the point.

She said it wasn't up to her. She said it in such a way that I understood I was not to ask any more questions. The job needed filling. Did I want to be the person to fill it? Yes I did. She introduced me to the cop as the guy I'd be partnered with. He wasn't talkative. In the few years that we worked together, I learned exactly nothing about him.

To get to the spot where the path started you took the exit, took a right turn past a gas station, rumbled over a set of old railroad tracks, and made another right turn that brought you right back up against hill leading to the barrier wall. The cop's waiting for us next to an old oak tree that'd been a lot smaller the last time I'd seen it. Still no car. Ashanda parks and gets out. She leaves her headphones around her neck and has the volume turned up.

His hands are empty and open at his sides. I imagine them holding, lifting, breaking. Ashanda keeps her distance and she never gets further away from the car than she is from him.

"Good to see you," I say. "Been a long time."

"The last time, you betrayed me." Coming from most people, it would have been too much. Like the guy from the mall

with his D&D books. Not from the cop. I don't think he was a cop, when he was alive. I don't know when he died, but I think it was a long time ago.

"I felt bad for the kid," I say. "I wanted to give him a break."

No answer. Doesn't mean shit to him.

Ashanda: "If you were fine with Gary being in charge, you would have let me get strangled."

The cop balls his hands into fists and looks down at the ground. "I thought anything would be better than the woman. But this needs to stop."

"Then let's hear it," Ashanda says.

One more long pause while he gets over the hill. "Gary enlisted me as soon as he took charge. He enjoys telling me what to do. He enjoyed explaining how he'd gotten rid of her."

Ashanda doesn't look away. "Tell me."

"Not yet."

"Why not?"

He takes a step forward and gestures down at his bare bloody feet.

"Your partner..." He draws the word out with sarcasm as he says it. "...left me like this. I'll tell you what I know. But not for free."

We leave. The cop gets in the back seat and Ashanda drives. She keeps her face hard right up until she turns her back on him, and then the curtain falls. A bead of sweat starts at her forehead and makes its way down to her chin.

We get back on the highway. We reach the top of a hill and see a neon cross standing tall from the top of a building over a mile away.

2

It's a big, big church. The parking lot looks like it belongs to a hospital or a stadium. The main way in is a bank of sliding glass doors, still shining under the floodlights at half past midnight.

The cop tells Ashanda to stop the car as we turn in. He stands on the grass, on the long elevated line next to the drainage ditch, near the road. That's as close as he's willing to get. Ashanda parks the car and approaches the pearly gates.

No handle, no doorbell. Ashanda waves her hand in front of the sensor and jumps up and down but nothing happens. There's a shiny tile floor on the other side of the door. It's almost silly how big a room it is. Maybe they think they'll need the space if another flood gets sent down.

Anyway, it's empty. Nobody there.

Ashanda is about to turn her back on the place when the doors slide open. She walks inside. There are five entrances to the auditorium, all big metal fire doors painted dark blue. The middle pair are open and there's music playing. I wonder if Ashanda has heard this song before.

"...you make everything... groovy..."

She walks into the auditorium and looks down at the stage. There are three big white-silver projection screens hanging from the rafters, each one facing a different pie slice. The speakers are big enough to live in, and the man on stage has them turned all the way up so that the room shakes. He's sitting in a folding chair on the stage, leaning back like he were on the beach, smiling and bobbing his head and tapping his toes to the music.

A few years can be nothing, or they can leave nothing behind. I have to look closely to see through the janitor's uniform and the beard and the twenty pounds, and even under all that it's hard to believe it's the same person. Mark with a K.

He sees Ashanda come through the door, waves hello, and reaches for the remote so he can turn down the volume.

"How's it going?"

Mark stands up, folds up the chair, and leans it carefully against the wall in back of the stage.

"You're with him, aren't you? I can kind of feel it in the air, I remember what it was like. You there, Charlie Harmer on WBLI?"

I don't want to step on Ashanda's play, but it seems rude to remain silent. Wrangling those big speakers stretches a muscle I didn't know I had.

"Classic radio. It's been a while. This is Ashanda. Ashanda, this is Mark."

"Nice to meet you." Ashanda didn't know where this was going. She didn't go hard or soft, she left it up to me. I was grateful, but it made me wish I knew more than she did.

"Likewise," Mark says. He reaches into his pocket and pulls out a silver car key. Light from the spotlights shine off of it. He holds it in front of him with two fingers.

"You're here about this?"

Ashanda doesn't say anything. He throws her the key and she catches it.

"There," Mark said. "All yours."

He sits down at the edge of the stage. His feet dangle like a kid at a restaurant.

I chime in. "The big guy made it sound like it wasn't going to be quite this straightforward."

"No, I'm done. It's the game we've been playing. I give him the key, there's nothing to stop him from coming up behind me some late night when I'm alone and tearing me apart. But I know that, so I keep the key hidden away, so if he hurts me he never gets it back. So nobody gets what they want.

"He keeps pulling haunted house tricks to let me know he hasn't gone away. I'm tired of the pounding on my door late at night and the bloody handprints. I thought the church would be a safe place, but it's all in his head. If you could just walk in here there's no reason he couldn't do the same thing. But I tripped and fell into a life here. People know who I am. I keep the place clean. I go to the service on Sunday morning and people thank me for doing such a good job. And I get to listen to whatever music I want all night long.

"I'm finished with it. No more secrets. You saved my life, or close enough. Whatever you want that thing for, it's all yours."

He lets himself fall back onto the stage. He looks up at the ceiling. He reaches for the remote.

"It's fine. You can go."

It takes Ashanda a while. Maybe she'd make it out faster if I could look her in the eyes, give her something to let her know that it's okay. But she takes her first step backwards, and then she turns around and leaves the auditorium. She hears the bells from the beginning of "Back In Black" shaking the building as she steps back out into the parking lot.

The cop is where he was before.

"He wants a truce," Ashanda says. She's standing on the concrete. He's on the grass, on the hill, above her. "You get the key if you promise to leave him alone."

"I don't believe you. I think he told you to give me the key."

"Why do you think that?"

"Because he's tired," the cop says. "Because he's weak."

Ashanda waits, thinks. Then she throws it over.

He catches the key with both hands and for a moment it looks like he's praying.

"You have no reason to hurt him. You got what you wanted."

"He stole from me."

"What does that matter now?"

The cop doesn't answer the question.

"I have an obligation to you."

He tells us what we want to know. The whole story. Then he turns his back on both of us. As he opens his hands a dark shape rises up out of the ground. When it takes its place, when it's his car again, he runs a giant hand over the hood, the same motion you'd use to pet a horse.

He opens the door to the car. Ashanda doesn't quite move to stop him.

"So what are you going to do?"

"I haven't decided," he says.

He climbs into the driver's seat and does a slow lazy U-turn onto the highway. He hits the gas and he's gone.

Ashanda slides her headphones down over her ears.

"We don't have to make the drive tonight," I tell her.

"Yes we do."

3

The sun's coming up by the time we make it to Alton. There's a weird little turn off the highway you have to take that makes you feel like you're in a pinball machine and just fell into the gutter. We make the turn and drive through the woods until they pull back to let us see.

The road is at a distance from the Mississippi. Between us and the water is a layer cake; there's the road, two pairs of train tracks, a stretch of brown and green grass with a bike path going through it, and then the river, which is wide enough that the other side is just a thin green strip from where we are. The water is rushing, the sky is clear.

There are a few red brick buildings along the side of the road on the way up. No signs, no windows. I have no idea what they are. As we make our way north, a factory looms over the horizon. From a distance, it looks like something from a cartoon, taller than it is wide.

And then, as we get closer, we see a giant pink boat, which is our destination. The parking lot is a triangle wedged in between the casino and the bridge that leads to St. Louis.

CHAPTER 14

1

Ashanda parked the car and headed on inside. The main entrance was a bridge with a bouncy wooden floor and a tight black canvas ceiling. On the other side was a station with a metal detector. A man in a uniform smiled at her and welcomed her to the casino. He asked for ID.

Ashanda told him she was here to play roulette. He told her that was great, and that he just needed to see some ID first. She repeated to him that he was she was here to play roulette. He was about to say something when she interrupted him and told him, for the third time, that she was here to play roulette.

He smiled and wished her good luck, no longer appearing to really see her. She went in.

There were three floors, one above and one below, plus an observation and smoking deck all the way at the top. The cashiers were near the entrance and the roulette wheel was downstairs. Ashanda bought some chips and went down. The early morning crowd were all entrenched at their slot machines. She could be dressed up like a bunny rabbit; she could be holding a gun.

An overweight woman in a pink sweatshirt was chasing a little girl who looked just like her in circles around a flower display, begging her nicely to please stop making a scene. The little girl started singing a song from a Pixar movie and kept running.

There was nobody by the roulette table. Ashanda waited in front of it for twenty minutes. She was tired. She closed her eyes for a moment, and when she opened them there was an elderly man with white hair and a pointed nose and a red vest standing behind the wheel.

"Bets," he said.

For a moment that seemed to go on for forever, Ashanda completely forgot what she was supposed to do. It came back to her out of nowhere. Seven on even, ten on seven, nine on nine, thirteen on black.

The old man spun the wheel. It went around, once, twice, three times. It got to the point where it should have slowed down, but it didn't.

The screens of the slot machines all went black. The people playing didn't seem to notice. They all stood up calmly, without saying anything, and filed towards the stairs like machines. Soon the bottom floor of the casino was empty except for her and the dealer.

The wheel kept spinning.

"Follow me," the dealer said, and came out from behind the table.

Ashanda followed him through the employee-only gate that led to the kitchen. To the right, just inside the curtain, was a metal door. If you weren't looking for it, you probably wouldn't notice that it was there.

The dealer unlocked the door and held it open. On the other side was a cramped spiral staircase, lined with red shag, going down. Ashanda went through and heard the door close and lock behind her. There were no lights and no windows, but it wasn't dark. Just bright red, all the way down. Further down than should have been possible on a boat.

The door at the bottom was just like the one at the top. Ashanda knocked and it opened. There was an orange room on the other side. Chairs around a boardroom table. Gary was in one of the chairs. He was wearing a white T-shirt and a pair of jeans. Opposite him was a beautiful woman with long brown hair.

The roulette dealer was sitting at the head of the table. To his left was the woman in the pink sweatshirt Ashanda had seen upstairs. To his right was that woman's daughter. The three of them had the same expression, held in the same way. Calm and professional, like the concierge at a hotel.

"Have a seat," the little girl said. Ashanda sat down at the foot of the table, where there were two chairs, squeezed in tightly next to each other.

Gary followed her with his eyes. A drop of blood fell from his chin down to the table.

"Both of you have a seat," the woman in the pink sweatshirt clarified.

Ashanda saw, and did not see. With her peripheral vision, she could feel Charlie sitting next to her. But when she turned her head towards him, he vanished. Not all the way- she could see an outline, his shoulders, the top of his head, his hands moving. But the moment she tried to think of how she might describe him to somebody else, there was nothing, he was gone.

"We have a lot to talk about," said the roulette dealer.

2

The cop's story had been pretty straightforward. The brunette had been the boss, but even the boss has a boss. She has laws to uphold, rules to follow, and consequences for not doing what she's supposed to do.

"We need to settle this. Once and for all," said the woman in the pink sweatshirt.

"We have more important things to be doing," said the child. "Other places to be."

The brunette didn't talk to them herself. That was one of the rules. You had a messenger. Gary had the cop. The brunette had Gary. Being the liaison was an unpleasant job, which was probably why Gary was the one assigned to it, but it did give you face time with the people in charge. Charlie and Ashanda still didn't know how Gary found out about the Ethan Pale situation. Maybe the brunette had enlisted his help with something, or maybe he'd heard about it some other way. Meredith wasn't the type to keep secrets.

The bottom line was, he found out. The boss had broken the rules. So he went to the boss's boss, and he put in a bid.

"So let's see if we can come to an agreement," said the dealer.

Ashanda tried to say something, but she couldn't. Her throat locked up like a bad elbow. She tried to stand up, but she couldn't do that either.

The child smiled. Gary rolled his eyes.

"Not how it works," Gary says. "People like us don't get to just talk to people like them."

Ashanda tried to ask but she still couldn't say anything. Nothing from Charlie either.

"To speak to us," the child said. "You have to pay for the privilege."

How, Ashanda couldn't say.

"Pain," Gary said. "Your own or other people's." Gary laughed. "I've been making down payments, but I don't know about you guys. This should be interesting."

A deck of cards appeared in the dealer's hands. The table got shorter, the room got smaller. The dealer put a single card down in front of each of them.

Ashanda got the jack of clubs. It was the only face card.

3

Ashanda was sitting in a restaurant, talking on her cell phone, leaving a message on her boyfriend's voice mail, her third in the last hour.

"I'm scared," she whispered. She was fourteen years old. She would rather have died than have a single other living soul hear her say that. "Please call me. I love you so much."

Her message ended with a beep. She put her phone on the table and waited and waited. The waitress brought her an ice cream sundae.

When she'd woken up in the motel room this morning he'd been gone but she knew he was going to come back. He had to come back.

4

She was back in the orange room. She wasn't going to cry, but she was right at the line, could feel something slipping.

"This is the first round," said the woman in the pink sweatshirt.

"What do you have to say?" asked the child.

Ashanda bit down on her lower lip hard before she said anything. "She didn't go through with it. If she lost her job because she was going to bring somebody back from the dead, either she couldn't or she decided not to. Either way, she didn't actually break the rule. And he did. He brought Ethan Pale back to life."

"That is a good point," said the roulette dealer.

"Second round," said the woman in the pink sweatshirt.

The dealer picked up the cards, shuffled twice, and dealt. Ashanda got a ten. The next highest card was Gary's eight.

5

Ashanda was back in the closet. She could hear her mother crying for help. The door wouldn't open. She couldn't breath.

It wouldn't stop.

6

It did stop. She was back in the orange room. She remembered this place. She couldn't think, but she had to. The woman in the pink sweater said something, but Ashanda only heard it a moment later.

"Say what you're going to say. We have no time to waste."

"Gary's having kids kill themselves for no reason. He had zombies stomp a guy at a restaurant. He..."

She tried to keep talking, but she was running out of air. She could feel the hand on her throat.

"We know about all that," the child said, smiling.

"Indeed we do," said the dealer. He didn't seem as happy about it.

"I don't know who Ethan Pale is, but I didn't bring anybody back from the dead. That's silly. You can do an audit if that's your idea of a good time but you won't find anything. As for the rest, I have an aggressive management style." Gary pointed his thumb at the brunette, who was still staring down at her lap. "I'm not going to do things exactly like she did."

"Third round," said the woman in the pink sweatshirt.

Ashanda got the ace of diamonds.

CHAPTER 14

1

"Fucking bullshit."

That's me. Ashanda's already gone. Her back is locked straight and her eyes are vacant.

At first I'm not sure why it is I can say anything. But I guess I've inflicted enough pain over the years to have a little extra in the tank.

"Those were the cards," the pink lady says. The kid smiles a perfect neener-neener smile and I want to drop her headfirst onto the table.

"Three times in a row."

"Those were the cards," the pink lady repeats.

"It happens," the dealer says quietly.

"If she gets it again, leave her alone. Do it to me instead." I speak without premeditation. I don't know what I'm saying until after I say it.

"That's adorable," Gary says. "But it's not the rules."

"If we were playing poker and I wanted to push a bunch of my chips over to somebody else I'd get looked at funny, but I wouldn't be breaking the rules."

Gary: "You're not playing poker."

"He can do a switch," the dealer says.

The pink lady: "Do we really want to let him do a switch?"

The kid laughs like she just stole a first grader's dessert at lunch. "Fine with me. I think that makes two."

The pink lady shrugs, the dealer doesn't do anything. He won, she lost.

Ashanda comes out of it and gasps for air. She tries to put her words together and she can't.

"You can talk for her, Charlie," the dealer says.

I get it out as fast as I can.

"The brunette made one mistake. Half a mistake, and how long did it take her to make it? You want stability, right? You want the trains to run on time. That's not Gary. I can't be telling

you anything you don't already know. What do you think he'll get up to if you give him a few decades to get comfortable?"

"I don't know, but I'm curious," says the kid. The other two look over at her and seem embarrassed.

Gary doesn't have anything to say. The dealer deals.

"Split pot."

Gary got a six of hearts. Ashanda and myself each get a black king.

"Switch."

Up and away I go.

2

I find myself in a one-bedroom apartment. Not a single thing here is good, or works properly, or is pleasant to look at. If there was an intelligence coordinating the set design of this place, then they overplayed their hand. The floor is dirty, there isn't any furniture, there's a draft coming from the windows, it smells.

The alternative, which I begin to favor, is that this is in no way an exaggeration, and that this is just what it was like.

There's a woman standing over me, then under me, as I cease to be Ashanda and become myself. She looks like a dragon inhaling, ready to go. Then she sees who it is. She doesn't deflate-she doesn't have to calm down because she wasn't actually angry.

She's a good actor. Like her daughter.

"The hell are you?"

"I'm Charlie. Ashanda's not coming."

She's confused.

"The voice said I was supposed to yell at her."

Again, I'm slow. I look for something in her inflection that isn't there. She was going to see her kid and now she isn't. That has to mean something. "Why would you yell at her?"

"The voice said I'd get privileges if I did."

Again I'm looking, and again I'm not finding. Hearing her voice, seeing her face, gets rid of any doubts that I might have had that this is Ashanda's mother.

And because I'm apparently very slow: "Ashanda's not coming."

And now she's confused, and I'm confused that she's confused, and only then does Charlie Harmer the keen observer of human behavior finally allow himself to realize that she doesn't actually give a shit.

She sees that I see. She gives me one last scan, to see if I might be good for something, and comes up empty. She pouts, turns her back on me, sits down on the floor, and leans back against the wall. For lack of a better course of action, I do the same thing on the opposite side of the room.

I'm looking at her, but she's not looking at me. I ceased to exist when she decided there wasn't anything I could do for her.

I shouldn't say a damn thing. I should take the hint.

"Ashanda's getting good grades. She wants to go to college."

Nothing. She doesn't even raise an eyebrow. She just sits there like I hadn't said a word.

We wait out the rest of the time, until we both are pulled back to where we came from. Even before today, I've seen things I had no reason to expect I'd ever see, maybe things I wasn't meant to see. Mysteries. But if you can explain to me how somebody like Ashanda comes from somebody like that, I'll take you to where Jimmy Hoffa's buried.

CHAPTER 15

1

Jack Harmer poured himself a rum and coke, then a ginger ale for Ashanda. He set her drink down in front of her gently, without getting any closer to her than he had to. He treated her like she'd just been in a car accident. No need to rush, even if he was a little confused. This wasn't what he'd been expecting.

She got it together to look around.

"Why are we in a bar?"

"I wanted to have a drink with my son."

He was upset. She did not want to upset him. It struck her insistently in a place beyond judgment. This is the guy, the one so many of the others she'd met over the course of her life were pretending to be. The man in the double-breasted suit in front of her was the genuine article and not to be fucked with.

Or made angry. But as it happened, if he was not angry it was not with her. He gave her that much for free, just by looking in her eyes. He was a gentleman. She was his guest, even if her presence happened to be a surprise.

"A voice told me that I was supposed to make him suffer, when and if he showed up. I was given a great deal of latitude when it came to making that happen. The understanding seemed to be that I was in the best position to figure out the details." He took a long sip. "I was promised rewards. Less time in the place where they pulled me from, more time doing other things."

Ashanda didn't want to ask. But there was nothing else to ask, and she knew she'd be just as uncomfortable saying nothing.

"Is that what you were going to do?"

"No. I lied to them. The fuck are they going to do to me they haven't done already?"

He took another drink. Ashanda took a sip too, in imitation of him, and felt belatedly ridiculous.

"You know him, then. Charlie."

Ashanda reached for surer territory. "I do. We work together."

"How is he?"

"All right, considering." She decided that she was speaking to a person who appreciated honesty. "He's dead. If you didn't know."

She immediately decided she'd made the right choice. He was sad, and still angry, but none of it was heading her way. "I didn't. Thank you for letting me know. There isn't a good way for me to keep track of time, in the place they usually keep me. It's been a while, hasn't it?"

"Yeah, I think so."

"You think so."

He took a close look at her for what she realized was the first time.

"I had a lot that I wanted to tell him. I've thought a lot about what I would say, given the opportunity."

"I'm sorry."

"You have nothing to feel sorry for."

"I don't mean that it's my fault. I'm just sorry that it's like this."

"Does my son trust you?"

Looking right at her, pinning her down. But when she looked back at him, soft eyes. Green eyes. She wondered if Charlie had them too.

"He hasn't had much choice," Ashanda said.

Jack thought about that. He came to a decision and pushed his glass to the side.

"I spent the last fifteen years of my life in prison. I don't think Charlie went more than a month without visiting me, the whole time. Even when I told him to stop, he wouldn't stay away. And he never gave himself any credit for it.

"So anything I say now, I could have told him then. Each time I saw him, I knew it might be the last time, and I kept my mouth shut. Even before I went in, I had all the time in the world.

And now that I'm the way I am now, all I do is think about what I would say, if I had just one more chance.

"And here's the moment and I still think I have a decision to make. I still think I have something to figure out.

"You just let somebody know you did a bad thing and don't say what it is, you enflame their imagination. You get bigger, not smaller. People start thinking of you like you're a movie star."

You're stalling. Ashanda didn't say it. He stopped talking, came back out of himself, saw her, read her mind. He steeled himself.

"When I was seventeen, I raped a girl that lived down the street from me. Me and two other guys. My buddies had known each other longer than they knew me, and I knew I was the one on the bubble, so when they wanted to do it, I said sure, Shirley lives over there, even if she tries to rat us, out nobody'll believe her, the way she is.

"When we got her alone, she tried to yell. I punched her in the face. I think I broke her nose. She shut up then.

"After that was when they started taking me seriously. At first it was just the bad guys, but all it took to get the good citizens of the world on my side, eventually, was a little silver in my hair and a tailored suit. Once I'd been around for a while, they all smiled at me when I walked down the street. Those others, they were the really scary ones. I was the one who kept them safe. And when they saw me, they got to live the dream a little bit. They got to imagine themselves in my shoes, doing whatever they wanted and looking good.

"That was the only way Charlie ever saw me. He never knew. He thought it was his idea to shoot that girl. He thought he was the worst person in the world, for taking the road that I'd paved for him. As if anybody else in the whole wide world wasn't capable of doing the same thing, if it was put in front of them on a menu like that."

If he'd told her this cold, Ashanda wasn't sure how she would've reacted. But she wasn't cold. She was numb. She wondered where she'd be, if she weren't here, and if that other place would've been enough to finish her off.

The easiest thing for her to do was to get ready for the next thing. She needed to arm herself.

"Where do you go when you're not here? What's it like?" Jack Harmer didn't say anything. Not for that question.

"Never mind," Ashanda said. "Answer this one instead. What would you have, if you could have anything? Leaving Charlie out of it. What do you want right now?"

He knew. She knew he knew. He didn't want to say it.

"I'm not just curious. And I think I know what you're thinking. Helping me is the same as helping Charlie right now, and I need this."

Jack Harmer thought about that. He finished the rest of his drink in one long sip.

2

Back in the orange room.

"I think we can settle this right now," Ashanda said.

Gary laughed. Fat, wet. "Is that what you think?"

She ignored him and addressed the three. She felt Charlie return to the seat next to her, but he didn't say anything. He swayed invisibly, a tree in the wind.

"You made a mistake when you put him in charge, but you're worried that the cure will be worse than the disease. You can't just pull him out and put somebody else in. That's one of the rules you all have to follow. That's why Gary had to get Ethan Pale to sign the contract. It's like buying stock to take over a company."

"You're not as stupid as you look," Gary said. "That's exactly what it's like. Except I wasn't dumb enough to sell any of my stock. Management can open up the bidding for the job, but I'm not going down as easily as some bitch with a boyfriend."

Ashanda focused on the woman in the pink sweatshirt.

"You want things to be orderly. You'd rather wait and see if Gary can get it together than start a war that might get out of control."

"Yes," the woman in the pink sweatshirt said. Yes, the sky is blue. Yes, the fork goes on the left and the knife goes on the right.

"So if you knew that Gary would sign over all of his power, immediately, right here at the table, the minute that you opened up bidding on the job, that would solve the problem. You wouldn't have any problem with that." Ashanda turned towards the dealer. "And you wouldn't either. That'd be a majority."

"It would be unanimous," the child said. "I have no idea what you're talking about. This is great."

The dealer nodded his head. He was listening.

Gary wasn't as cocky as he'd been a moment ago. He was listening too.

Charlie: "What do you have in mind?"

3

Ashanda's idea required one last bending of the rules, but it was a small price to pay to get things back to normal. Gary had a last request. The seven of them headed up the stairs, through the casino, up to the smoking deck. Nobody saw them as they went. Every single person in the casino was sitting at a slot machine. The machines weren't turned on, the screens were black, but still they just sat there, relaxed and perfectly still. The sun was coming up.

Gary sat at the bench by the railing and watched. From where they were, if you didn't look too far in either direction, the river might as well be an ocean.

"People talk about how great this is supposed to be," Gary said. "I don't fucking get it. It's orange. Then it's blue. Who gives a shit?"

A few years later, when she was finally in the mood to think about all this, Ashanda did some reading on Gary. Any public library with a shelf on serial killers would have a book or two on him; he reliably came in second to John Wayne Gacy. Gary'd had the kind of early childhood you might expect; getting placed in a foster home had only been a marginal improvement. He'd been bullied in school, he'd gotten discharged from the Navy. Nobody was really sure when he started killing people, but one of the more common theories was that he'd tried a couple of times to pick up younger men and gotten turned down hard. He'd gotten caught after three years. Then death row. Then a needle.

Once Ashanda had made her proposal, Gary'd laughed and started talking about "the O-word". He said it as much as he could, usually to either Ashanda or the brunette. Over and over again. He licked his lips when he did it, or at least the place where his lips should have been.

The sunrise was over. "Well, fuck this then. It's been fun, kids. Give me the contract."

The roulette dealer produced a piece of thick manila stationary from his inside jacket pocket. He gave it to Gary, along with a red pen. Gary signed the paper and dropped the pen. He flipped off the sun with both hands. "Ready when you are."

The three of them made a simultaneous motion with their hands, like they were plucking a mosquito out of the air. Gary vanished. He did not pass on. He was not transformed from one thing into another.

He was no more. O stood for oblivion.

There wasn't much else to say. The brunette departed as soon as the contract was signed, and whatever it was that let Ashanda know where Charlie was had stopped working as soon as they'd stepped outside. The trinity led Ashanda back down to the casino entrance.

"Thank you so much for your good work," the dealer said. He seemed to mean it. "Never come back here. Never set foot on this boat again. Do you understand?"

Ashanda said that she did and the three of them were gone.

Ashanda walked back over the bridge to shore. There was a bed and breakfast a short drive east of the casino. They had a vacancy. Her remaining cash was enough to pay for two and a half days, minus twenty dollars to pay for a meal on her drive home. The lady that owned the place was nice and gave her the third night because she paid cash up front and seemed to be in a jam.

Food, sleep.

CHAPTER 16

My goodbyes with Ashanda were a little awkward. She didn't want me to feel like she wanted me gone, but she wanted me gone. I didn't blame her for that. The Emerald City hadn't been anybody's idea of a good time and it seemed reasonable for her to want to get back to Kansas as soon as possible.

We did have a little time to get everything squared between us. She told me a little about my dad. She said that he was supposed to be the one to kick my ass when I got dealt the high card, but that he wasn't going to do it, no matter what the consequences were. And that he missed me.

I told her that I'd seen her mother and that the same was true of her. I hope I'm a better liar than Ashanda.

The last thing I made clear to her is that if she ever needed my help, she should reach out. I don't have a phone number, but if she ever puts the word out there, it'll get to me eventually. And I'm not the only one. My kind of people talk, and we don't forget. Wherever she goes, from now on, Ashanda will have friends.

And that was it for us.

Shortly afterwards, I have a meeting with the brunette. We have lunch at Jim's Downtown Steakhouse, on Jefferson Street in the great city of Peoria. It's a nice place and you should go if you have the chance.

There are things the boss does and does not want to talk about, and the circumstances behind her losing her job are unambiguously in the second category. In the first are what she owes and to whom.

"Promises were made to the girl you saw at the table with me. College money. There wasn't an exact figure but I don't think we should be stingy."

The brunette emphasizes that this is not something she'll be making a habit of, but given the circumstances she agrees with me. She's a lot less generous when it comes to the rest of our coalition. I tell her that it wasn't just me who saved her bacon, but she doesn't want to hear it.

"This will not be a time for gratitude. It doesn't matter who did what. I'm back. It'll be the best thing for everyone if there's no confusion about that."

"You're worried that all the crazy might be giving people ideas."

"I'm not worried about anything. I'm aware of the problems I will be dealing with and I understand that I can't afford to let every other person I work with think that I have an obligation to them. I owe one favor to you personally. That is all."

"Two favors," I tell her.

She stops eating her salad. She is completely still, and for a moment her eyes are like two black holes, and I am allowed to think that I've made a terrible mistake.

Then she smiles. Lazy and sweet. Still not taking any shit.

"You make me laugh, Charlie. Fine. Two favors. What do you have in mind?"

"The first one's more of a suggestion. You've given me a lot of different jobs in the past, doing a lot of different things. But this whole fiasco has made it clear to me that there's more going on behind the scenes than I was familiar with. In the future, if there's work to do that's less pleasant but needs doing, maybe you'll consider me."

"You want more responsibility?"

"'I think 'want' would be putting it too strongly. But if there's heavy things to carry, I'm willing to pick them up."

She looks me over, still smiling.

"Consideration. That much you have. What's the other favor?"

CHAPTER 16

Alton had a lovely public library, and it was a fun town to walk around in. There were steep hills and antique stores and pawn shops. There wasn't so much to do that Ashanda felt bad that she was never going to come back, but the time she spent she enjoyed.

The day after she finished at the casino, she got Betty on the phone. Betty and Carol had hit the road when things got bad and went to stay with a mutual friend in Florida. When Ashanda said that the coast was clear, Betty suggested that maybe Ashanda's unplanned vacation could go on for another week or two so she could come join them. Ashanda said that she wanted to go home first and see how she felt.

She drove.

Cows, windmills, farmhouses.

She knew she was being stupid. She didn't think the car was going to get reported stolen, but she still had no license and no insurance. It would be a lot smarter and safer to leave the car in a parking lot near an Amtrak station, wipe it for fingerprints, and take the train back home. And yet here she was, driving.

Trees, standing alone, surrounded by green and brown and yellow fields that stretched out as far as the eye could see in every direction.

She stopped at a gas station and saw a flier for an Ethan Pale show in the window. He was playing at a bar Friday night.

She was about an hour away from home when she remembered that she hadn't eaten yet. All of the sudden, she was hungry. She got off at the next exit. Her hands moved by themselves. There were closer restaurants and they all looked fine and Ashanda wasn't picky, but for some reason she let them go by, and even when she wasn't all that close to the highway anymore, she kept on going. By the time she started to wonder what she was thinking, she was surrounded by warehouses and fences, rolling over train tracks. When she finally came to a big intersection she saw that she was passing 47th Street. She was back in the city. Not that far from where she used to live.

She turned right, turned left. There was a restaurant wedged in between a garage and a place that bought scrap metal. She parked the car and went in.

The inside of the restaurant was a trapezoid; the eating area was a skinny triangle, two tables against the window facing the street and a row of stools by the counter that marked the edge of the kitchen. The interior had been put together more than fifty years ago and barely touched since. It wasn't retro; it was just old. White tile, a glowing sheet for a menu with black plastic letters that hadn't been rearranged in a long time.

On the far wall next to the bathroom was a framed picture of a skinny elderly white man with a big pair of black plastic glasses and a huge nose.

"That's a great man you're looking at. A visionary."

Ashanda turned towards the man behind the counter. He was wearing a white apron and had his long arms stretched out and his palms facing up.

"His vision was fairly modest as these things go, but let's give him some credit."

The man behind the counter had a shaved head and his name tag said his name was Samson, which immediately had Ashanda on the verge of cracking up. The mustache didn't hurt either.

"He's not in the room, Samson. I know he's your boss, but you don't have to suck up to him if he's not here. You could tell if he was, his nose would block out the sun."

They both stopped, a moment of mutual recognition between smartasses.

"You have me at a disadvantage."

"I'm Ashanda. Pleased to meet you."

"Likewise, Ashanda. Can I fix you some food, young lady?"

She ordered a hamburger. They talked about the man on the wall. He had a long Polish last name that Ashanda wasn't about to try to pronounce herself. He'd passed away a few years ago. Ashanda tried to apologize for making jokes, but Samson wouldn't let her.

"You should hear the shit he used to say about me. He was a mean old man and he liked to box. He was also a good guy so long as you looked at what he did and not what he said, but he'd dish it out if he thought you could take it."

Samson talked about him over the grill. Samson had saved up money for two years to buy a partnership in the restaurant, and then when the old man had died a year and a half later it turned out he'd left him the place in his will anyway, along with everything else that he had. The mortgage on the restaurant was such that it wasn't as good a deal as you might think, but Samson still appreciated it.

"I still don't get it," Samson said. "I knew he didn't have any family, but still. Didn't see that one coming. I've been talking about myself a lot, haven't I?"

Ashanda watched Samson while he cooked. He was older than he'd appeared at first glance. One of those that guys who didn't have time to slow down, but if he let his hair grow out she wouldn't expect all of it to come back. Then again, he probably wasn't going to let his hair grow out, so there you go.

Ashanda told him that a girl she knew had made a stupid decision over a boy and that she'd had to take a little trip to help her deal with the consequences.

"Good on you. Goodness knows I've been there."

"You let women make you stupid?"

She'd meant it as a joke, but he thought it over and seemed to take the question seriously.

"It's tempting for me to make it sound like I've lost count because I'm such a natural-born lover and they can't keep away from me. But really it was just the one."

"When was that?" Ashanda didn't know why she was asking. She worked it and made it seem like she didn't care, but she did, a lot, and she didn't know why that was either.

"A little over fifteen years ago." Samson had a moment too. He looked over his shoulder at Ashanda, once quickly. Trying to figure something out that he couldn't name. "She skipped out on me before the consequences got any worse than my car and the money I had around my place, but it could have been a hell of a lot worse. I was an idiot, when I was around her. I can see that clear as day now. I still think about her all the time, though." Serving Ashanda her food. "Isn't that crazy?"

"You were in love." Ashanda took a big bite. She'd paid twice as much for burgers that weren't half this good.

"I must have been. Only love makes you that stupid. Anyway. You're a student, Ashanda?"

They talked for a while, long after her meal was finished. She put her money down on the counter. She got up to leave, but she didn't leave. She looked at Samson. Samson looked at her.

"This is going to sound funny," Samson said. "But I've got a strong feeling that we've got more to talk about."

"I think so," Ashanda said. "Can I come back some time?"

"I hope you do. I'll be here. I always am."

"Good meeting you, Samson."

"Likewise, Ashanda."

Ashanda left the restaurant and felt his eyes on her back as she went. It was getting dark.

She put her hand on her car door and let it rest there. She closed her eyes and tried to see if there was anything in the air around her to notice. She wasn't sure if there was.

"Thank you, Charlie," she said. "I appreciate it."

She waited to see if there was going to be an answer. She didn't get one. She opened her eyes, laughed, and wondered if she was going to go crazy now, talking to people that weren't there and couldn't hear her. She got back into the car and drove north towards the expressway.

She had nothing to worry about. I could hear her just fine.

Many thanks to my buddy Derek Gettys of the Arson Club for his insights into the life of a traveling musician. All mistakes and misinterpretations are entirely my responsibility.

Also thank you a million times to the lovely people on my Patreon. Without you guys, none of this would be happening:

Tom Tancredi

Rob Detzner

Dan Detzner

Drew Detzner

Jonathan Hadley

Lorraine Ochoa

Sarah Detzner

Pain Strumpet

Ami Agner

Alice Liddell

Sheila Johnson

Brandon Sichling

Georgianne Detzner

Wesley Wong

Phil Schwartz

Joining my Patreon is the cheapest, fastest, best way to get your hands on all the new books I've got coming out, including new Charlie stories and a lot of other stuff too. You can check it out here:

https://www.patreon.com/detzner

And you can join my mailing list here to be the first to hear about everything I've got going on:

https://www.subscribepage.com/m3n5f2

Hope you liked the book. Thanks for being a reader. More good stuff coming.